I0822704

KAREN KOOKS

The Secret of Adrian

Book I

and

The Bright Desert

A Novel

ISBN: 978-1-67800-624-2

The Darwar

Northern Village
Northem Tower
Sarhat
Great Islands
Road to the northern village
South Sea
Dwinerd
South Forest
Spirit
South Tower
Warm Desert
Arishta

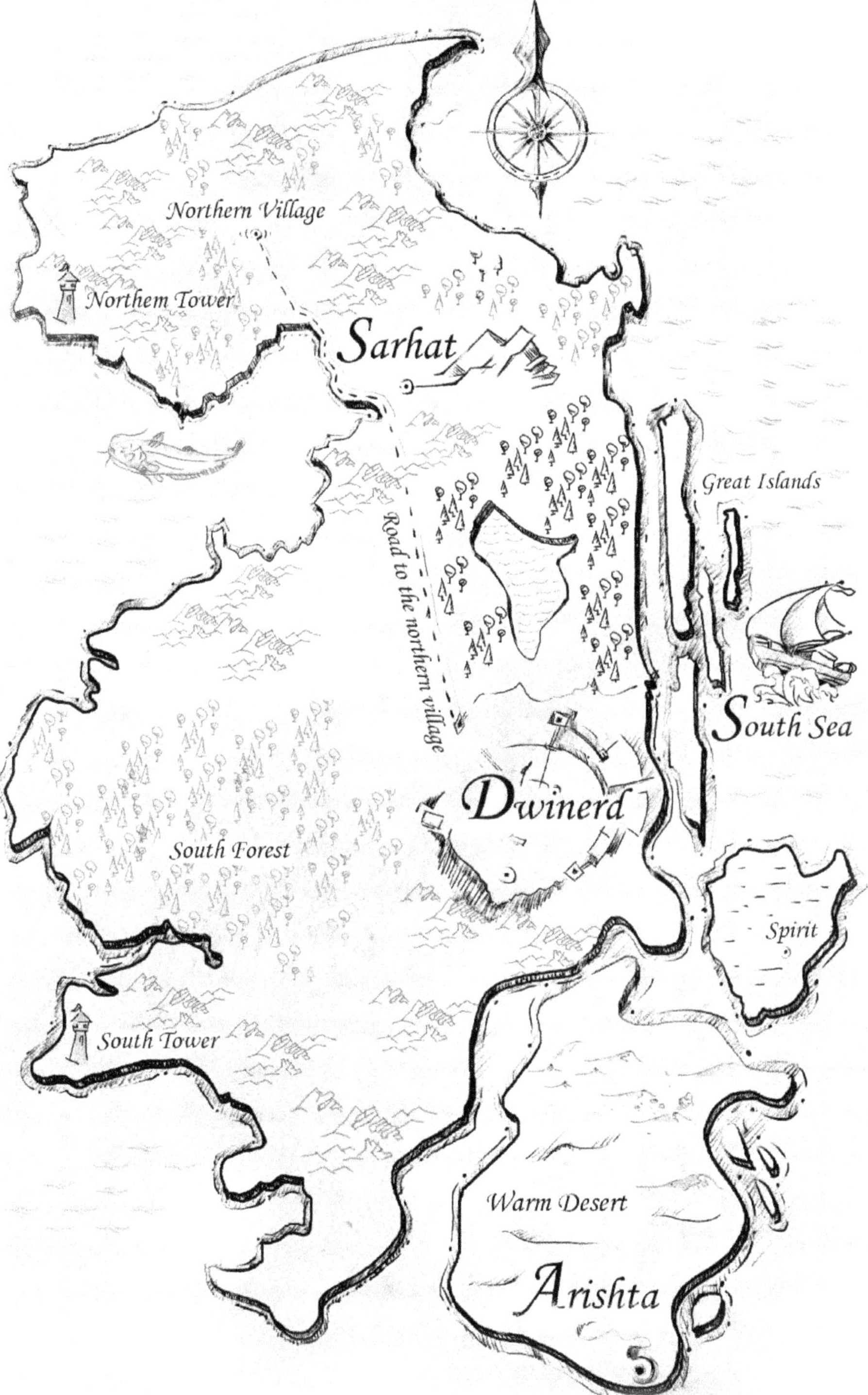

And the day will come
when the light will show you the way

CONTENTS

The Bright Desert

CHAPTER I
Union of Experts

••••

Ralph's University

There was an iron door at the farthest end of a dark corridor, which hardly was lightened by the rays coming out from it. An outline of a candle was visible from a small window on the door, which was shaped in the burning fire. The old man removes the candle with a special tool from the fire, cleans it with a piece of fabric and makes sure that the candle got its final shape from all sides and then fixes it on a small antique cart and heads to the gathering room.

"Hello, dear council! Our meeting for today was not planned and in general no one should know about this meeting," said the old man, who was the head of Ralph's University Council of connoisseurs, called Dargen.

"Something inexplicable is going on in our city, which is out of our science, I was informed today about that phenomenon, and that is why I invited you all here for a meeting."

The room was shaded and all connoisseurs were sitting around the round table, following Dargen's words attentive but a little frightened. There was the special candle in the midst, which was lit during the Great Gathering of connoisseurs and if the room was illuminated good and was working for a long time the gathering was over, and if it was otherwise, the danger was inevitable and the experts had a reason to think about, so the candle had an important meaning.

"The guards have recorded very bright flashes of lights in the southern part of the city, even in the darkest corner of the Darwar." He pauses for a moment and smoking from his old pipe, "In the mountains of Sarhat!"

"In Sarhat ?!" Everybody exclaimed startled.

"Yes!" Said Dargen while smoking his pipe again.

"But no one can enter there, even the guards. We all know very well what is going on in Sarhat," insisted one of the connoisseurs whose name was Vam, after Dargen he was the connoisseur, who was working the longest in the council.

"Maybe there were just thunderstorms, surely the weather has been gloomy recently," said Randolph, the youngest of the connoisseurs, who was asking most of the questions.

"Thunderstorms?" sniggered Vam,
"There is lightning in our area - Dwinerd, but not in Sarhat! Even the dust has no power in Sarhat to rise, neither will lightning could illuminate the territory."

"What could have caused the light there in that case?" Randolph said.
Dargen, one eye in the smoke of the pipe, was attentively following the discussion of the

connoisseurs trying to understand the possible ways of finding out the problem and suddenly the light of the candle started to fade. Right, at that time no voice was heard, but each fading of the candle seemed like a thunderbolt and everybody stopped speaking and looked at Dargen.

"Enough! That's all for today." He continued while following carefully from time to time fall of the candle.

"Go! And study that phenomenon, we will meet in the next discussion."

Dargen approached the candle, which was dimming from time to time and the light was reflecting on Dargen's face once burning light and then fading and intensifying the fear of the connoisseurs and at that time the silence seemed louder than the atmosphere in the room at the time of dim candle and Dargen put out the candle looking at it carefully.

—————— •••• ——————

When the council left, Dargen headed to the General Archives, where all historical information about the University and the city was kept. After a long search and exploring of old books, Dargen couldn't find anything useful and decided to go to the Special Library of connoisseurs. At the entrance Darry - a guard was waiting for him. She was a middle - aged woman with long hair and very fine features. Dargen said, approaching Darry.

"Hello Darry!" Dargen said clearly.

"Hello, dear Dargen."

Noticing that Darry was staring at him, he continued abruptly.

"Can you bring me all the references about the lights?"

"Of course! right now." Darry brought all the materials to Dargen without any odd movement and questions.

"Thank you," Dargen took the materials without any odd word and started studying them right on Darry's desk in a hurry.

"Mister Dargen, you look very worried," Darry said, approaching Dargen and softening her voice as she continued,

"Is anything wrong?" Concluded Darry from hurrying Dargen's confused state.

"No, darling," answered Dargen absorbed in materials as he continued.

"Everything is fine, just there are many things that interest me as an old man." As he found the part in the materials that interested him, he headed to the exit forgetting his pipe on the desk. Darry took the pipe and hurried after Dargen.

"Mister Dargen, your..." She hardly finished her words as Dargen left the room and when Darry came back to the papers noticed written there.

"*And the day will come when the light will show you the way.*" Not understanding anything she started gathering the papers.

Sarhat

Dargen was walking up a rising mountain. The whole city was visible in the clouds from that height, the mountain was so high that the peak could not be seen and behind which dark forests were formed and were so dense that even the brightest sun rays were so difficult to reach by the sun, and for a moment he stopped and looked straight at the mountain and exclaimed.

"I know you're here!" the wind shook Dargen's clothes quietly, touching his beard as if it was a single body. And after an unusual silence, a silhouette of a man was approaching from the deep of the mountain appeared very slowly, with a worn-out piece of clothing on him, from which his face was very difficult to see.

"I thought you hadn't forgotten my name," said the approaching man from afar, continuing to draw closer and continued almost reaching Dargen.

"Actually, you forgot!" There was a smile on his face, but that smile was no ordinary smile. There was an emotion of hard times absorbed in it, which seemed a smile from the first side, but as there was no other way to express that feeling, he was involuntarily smiling.

"Valmar! I have something to talk to you," Dargen said quietly.

"Something to talk about? Hmm…, Dargen himself," said Valmar walking closer as he continued,

"Something to talk about, when we met last time, as far as I remember you didn't have."

"That's enough, Valmar, I…" Valmar interrupted Dargen and continued raising his voice.

"That's enough! That was your every second word. I was so tired of your enough's. You think you are the most knowledgeable and that all the experts of the world have something to learn from you, and who has now come to whom?" Valmar was saying while going around Dargen.

"You know, that I wouldn't come, but…" Dargen said while following Valmar's moves.

"But the lights started to worry you," continued Valmar with Insightful look standing right in front of Dargen.

"Yes, and I know, that you're aware of what it's about," looking at Valmar's eyes for a moment, he continued.

"I hope that's not what I imagine."

"And maybe it's just that," Valmar answered in a low voice and with a smile.

"Valmar!" Dargen exclaimed,

"It's not all that simple, I don't know what you think, but you can't let it happen in our time and on our land," When Dargen was angry at him, the wind seemed to get stronger.

"On our land?" Valmar sniggered and continued.

"More precisely, on your land! That land is not mine for a long time now, this is mine, we are here under your leadership, though it is the only thing for which I am grateful to you, I think it's more important, true, we are cut off from everything, but we have our own, I think it's more important," said Valmar calming down and gazing at the view of the city that opened in front of him.

"Has it already happened?" Asked Dargen staring at Valmar.

"What will my answer give you, anyway, you already know?"

"I want to make sure." This time Dargen approached Valmar.

"Since when Dargen started needing to make sure?" Valmar replied turning and continued,

"You are weakening my friend."

"This time, that power is beyond me and I can't understand."

"Something that needs to happen, will happen." And looking again toward the view from the mountain to the city.

"Valmar! What happened between us-is our fight, but this…"

"What's that? What is the difference? I even forgot what we were fighting for, I've lived most of my life in this dark corner, cut off everybody and now that it's time for me to live you want to disturb me?"

"Nothing would disturb you, if you didn't choose the path that led you here. I have held you back many times from that path, you know it very well."

"Of course, if my ideas at your noble university were not considered evil, I might as well be one of those connoisseurs now and in the city of connoisseurs," said Valmar laughing and continued.

"Now we have our city and your connoisseurs even are afraid of looking towards it, Sarhat is a district that doesn't exist for them, but here we also have such connoisseurs and believe more clever and more powerful than them."

"It's not important who's more powerful, it's important, what your power serves to." Dargen answered clearly.

"Yes, you are right as always, but you are not provident!" Telling Dargen these words, Valmar looked at Dargen's eyes very closely and continued,

"You are afraid!" Then he turned back and quietly headed toward the dark forest.

"Valmar..." Dargen said anxiously and followed as Valmar was going back to the side of the dark mountain.

"Valmar!" Said Dargen again, but this time louder, and Valmar slowed down his steps, taking a deep breath as he whispered without looking back. "Adrian."

CHAPTER II

The Stranger

••••

Dwinerd | City of Experts

Dwinerd was the oldest city of Darwar and inhabited by many experts, where experts were born or would become and where Ralph's University was situated, the council of which consisted of five connoisseurs and ten members. To become a member, one had to overcome a very difficult and long path, then either become a connoisseur or not, because only those who had practical progress in addition to theoretical knowledge could get a position of a connoisseur. Besides practicing science, the members also were studying architecture, history, and a wide variety of other subjects, as the connoisseurs had many problems and they were responsible for the security of the inhabitants and to resist all kinds of evil. They were doing numerous researches and had to have endurance experience as well, and every two years they had an opportunity to submit their candidacy to the Council of Connoisseurs, where the connoisseurs and the leader of the University either would accept the application or would not depending on the achievements of the applicant. People from all over the world were coming to study and exchange experiences, as besides the members and connoisseurs, there was also a school, where you could become a member after graduating and serve to the University or become an independent specialist. The doors of Ralph's University were open to everybody, where people had to work hard to become the best. There were various laboratories at Ralph's University, where both general-purpose products and accessories for the University were produced, these included chandeliers, candles, chairs, truth vials, and many more. There were many legends about the truth and accuracy of the candle of the meeting of the connoisseurs, and none of the connoisseurs had an answer to it, as they couldn't understand themselves what kind of power was guiding the candle, there were just specific preparation mechanisms, that had been mentioned in books for centuries. Once upon a time, there was an alchemist whose name was Ralph, and in addition to being able to invent a variety of inventions, he was also able to unite around him many alchemists and connoisseurs and was able to eliminate the centuries-long hostility with his worthy discoveries and to use the information received from them for one purpose- for the benefit of the people and the state. It is said, that the main inventions connected with both the candle and the specially-illuminated chandeliers came from him, but the forms of their implementation were preserved partially, which were for general use, but the inventions of special significance were kept in one book, the place of which no one knew and all the connoisseurs were just dreaming of finding that book to be able to master these inventions. Ralph had also invented a destructive torch, which spared nothing and burnt whatever would appear ahead of it.

The young expert, Adrian, and his friend were standing near one of the poorest houses in the Dwinerd fair, waiting for the preparation of the fluid that Adrian needed to perform a new experiment and heal Hanna. Here you would see many on horseback, hurrying somewhere as the fair was booming with various adventures. The dirty and muddy street was full of garbage that was the output of the operating fair and it was a means of living for the poor and needy dwellers. The district by the fair has always been happy to welcome hopeless villagers coming from different places to the city, to use their labor force, snatch the last pence and throw them out to one of such dirty and muddy streets to continue the pitiful existence in the garbage of the fair.

"You don't know what has happened yesterday evening," said Dan. He was young doctor Adrian’s friend, who was a magician.

"And what?" said Adrian stepping back of the following horse to avoid the mud.

"There was a Great Gathering at Ralph's University and they say that there wasn’t such a big gathering for a long time already," said Dan very pleased with himself.

"I am always amazed at your possibilities of finding information!" Adrian answered.

"Of course! How can it be without it?" Dan said, looking around as he continued,

"There are rumors that strange creations of lights happen in the city, and Dargen was personally concerned about it and they gathered on that occasion."

"Lights in this dark city? I think it is a reason to rejoice not to worry," Adrian was joking.

"Another important event has happened, do you want me to tell, but on one condition, that we will drink in addition to today's laboratory tests."

"And what has happened?" asked Adrian indifferently, as he was more interested in the fluid they came there for.

"The candle, around which the experts gathered, faded during the discussion!" At this expression, the silhouette of a stranger at a distance stunned them, then disappeared as another horse passed.

"Did you notice!?" Adrian said as he continued,

"I don’t believe!"

"You should believe," Dan answered confused.

"What if these connoisseurs got so old, that their eyes faded, but not the candle?" Both laughed as the small window on the door by which they were standing opened and a hand appeared with a strange liquid-filled glass flacon, Adrian took that glass flacon carefully, then put gold medals behind it.

Taking the liquid-filled flacon, the boys made their way to the street and suddenly a range of horses passed and the young doctor collided with a man and the flacon fell out of his hand.

"Mister! be more attentive, please!" Adrian said confused, taking the liquid-filled flacon from the ground and examining the strange figure in front of him, whose face was almost fully covered.

"Maybe I was too attentive," the stranger said, approaching the man and stopping for a moment, while both looked at each other.

"There's nothing to worry about, let's go," Dan said, looking back and forth not to be a victim of others' attention and pulling his friend's hand.

"I just wanted to know where is this product from?" The stranger said, looking at the strange content of the flacon in their hands, that almost broke and could be mixed with the muddy colors of the street, as he continued.

"It is hard to find such strange contents."

"It's not your business!" Dan said confused as he continued,

"It's just colored water, nothing serious."

"Hmm..., You wouldn't keep the colored water so secretly," The stranger spoke without interference and with strange calmness,

"I just wanted to offer my support, I live right next to this house, on the second floor and I have different types of fluids, if you need, I can share it with you."

"No! We don't need anything." Dan said, turning to Adrian, who was glancing that mysterious image of the stranger,

"Let's go!"

"Anyway, if you change your mind, I am always here," the stranger continued as he moved forward,

"Ask for the stranger and they will guide you," he concluded as he left.

"And what's your name?" Adrian shouted after him as a horse passed in front of them, after which the young men lost the silhouette of the Stranger.

"Who was that stupid one, he scared us, what if we got caught?!"

"He didn't look like a catcher anyway, he looked more like the one to be caught," Adrian said and they set on horseback as they got to the end of the fair and moved on.

——— •••• ———

Adrian's house was not far from the central tower of Dwinerd, to get there one had to go by the bridge about a hundred meters to reach it, then you would appear on a hill, where a small two-story house was built, which had also a basement, where Adrian was doing his experiments.

"The whole city is talking about Hanna's disease, that the treatment is not possible, but I have a different view, today I found what I needed! I will merge the final elements and everything will work out, we should gather today and heal that girl!" Adrian said to his dog, heading to his lab leading to the basement. The dog was walking confidently beside him and as if understanding him, was growling next to him.

"I do it to protect my children in the future, so if there is danger, I will be able to heal them!" He stared at the dog as they both stopped for a moment and the dog put his tongue back closing his mouth.

"Yes, Wil! I have no children, but I will have one day, right?"

The lab was not very big, but there were all possible conditions to do experiments, there were many windows that looked to the side of the hill from where it was the path leading to the fair. There was a table in the middle, on which he was laying his patients, and there were different liquid-filled flacons, that almost nobody in the city had and if anybody knew about their existence, he could be brought to justice, but it didn't scare him, he was more scared of being helpless of the newly created problem, Hanna's disease, that had no explanation and nobody could help that girl. After working for a long time the Stranger as if appeared to him, who didn't introduce himself and he could not get the man out of his mind.

"What an indifference!" Adrian said angrily and continued as he threw the content of the fluid mixes into the trash.

"It should work out!"

The dark night was already near, and the rain was beginning to pour everywhere, and the thunder was so loud that it seemed to accentuate the gloom of the moment and gave the final chords of Hanna's sickness. An obscure disease in the city of connoisseurs entered into Eisenstoff's house, everybody knew about Eisenstoff's daughter's illness and many insisted that if not that night, the seventeen-year-old girl would surely die in the morning. All the doctors in the city tried to treat the girl, as well as invited professors from Ralph's University. Dr. Francis Block, a respected man at Ralph's Council, in particular, after examining the girl told the girl's father that the condition was hopeless and that excruciating fever of Hanna's body had no explanation, so any intervention was meaningless and impossible.

"Do you say there is no other way to heal her?" Hanna's father asked frustrated.

"Yes, sir! the medicine I have given only alleviates the fever, but it does not cure. Here we need something else, but the methods we know will not cure her."

After staying silent for a moment, Hanna's father continued.

"And where is the young man who said he knew how to help her?"

"Who? That offal!?" Block said stately,

"Mister, he has not even come here today, how can you believe in his words? He is just a nomadic doctor, who doesn't even know your place. It's not in vain, that people gave him the title of a deceiver." Block said satisfied with himself as he finished his words and looking at Hanna's helpless body once again, which was still struggling with the disease.

——— •••• ———

Once more making sure of the negative effects of the liquids, Adrian decided to go to the stranger, as the night had already come, and Hanna's illness had no chance to wait. Coming out of the larger double-sided window on the right beside the middle table, the curtains of which were coming in from the wind, as if to create a tendency to come out, he made his way down to the fair descended the stone path directly towards the fair by pillars coming out of stone. Crossing the city fair threshold, Adrian arrived at the Stranger's house. Climbing up the stairs made of worn-out stones, there was a large antique wooden door in front of Adrian, with iron embroidery and strange ornaments that did not repeat on any door of the district. Adrian paused for a moment, but as the lightning rumbled, he jumped up and the door in front of him moved back and sharing one side to the right wall, and the other to the left wall and a long corridor opened, with torches hanging on both sides of the wall and illuminating the corridor. Moving forward, Adrian noticed on the walls sketched maps of different regions, and making around fifty steps, he reached the intersection of corridors.

"That's it! The walk is over," Adrian said confused, sharply turning to look at an old man with a strange torch in his hand, that appeared in front of him.

"Oh, God! there is a man in this house!" Adrian exclaimed, somewhat joking.

"Yes, Mr. Adrian, please follow me," suggested the old man very politely, dressed in a dark red suit.

"Hmm..., okay," said Ad, confused and full of questions.

They continued their way to the left side of the corridor, which was illuminated and only the old man's torch lit up the area. Upon reaching the nearest staircase, they met a door that also had iron ornaments and opened strangely. The old man put a torch on the door and the door opened, the room behind it was very bright, and Adrian noticed that the light inside that door was not illuminating the corridor.

"This is probably a trick?" Adrian asked the old man and turned, noticing that there is nobody,

"What a hospitable house!" Ad said surprised and noticed a window with open curtains as he moved, there was pouring rain and the Stranger was standing in front of the window, who was looking outside and the lightning was outlining its silhouette.

"Welcome! my friend, please come in," Guiding Adrian to a round table that had strange figures put on it and the stranger also joined the table.

"Tricks with light are well developed in this house," Adrian said, looking back and forth,

"It would be good to have something like that in my lab!" he continued jokingly.

"Light is the most important meaning in this house, but I think you're interested in something else," said the Stranger in a deep voice.

"Yes, I need a liquid that I can use to overcome the fever, as long as I can remember you told me that you have many such things,"

Adrian said as he moved one of the figures and attentively looked at the stranger's silhouette.

"Yes, you are right. Larry!" said the Stranger, exclaiming. The old man's name was Larry, who brought with him two glassy flacons which one filled with liquid and the other was empty,

"Here is that liquid!"

"So easy," Adrian said, smiling and excited.

"Well, getting is always easier than making it," the Stranger continued quietly.

"You know how much I strove to get it, and now it has just appeared in front of me in a moment," he said as he put the figure in its place and preparing to take out the gold medals of his pocket.

"Yes, you are right," said the Stranger following Adrian, who continued to pull the gold out of his pocket,

"You know, I am a scientist myself, and I no longer need money, and I am more interested in experiments and I see the meaning of my life in it," he continued after a moment of silence.

"I need blood! for this flacon."

"Blood?" Adrian asked in surprise.

"Yes, blood!" the Stranger continued,

"Don't be afraid my friend! Nobody will harm you here, I take the blood sample from people very little to do laboratory work for creating such liquids in the future," indicating the fluid for which Adrian came.

"And how should I give it to you?"Ad continued.

"There's nothing difficult. Larry has a needle, with which you can very easily tap your finger and pour a few drops of blood into this empty flacon, after which I'll give you this liquid."

"You are doing strange experiments, sir," said Ad, standing and looking toward the rain from the window.

"Those strange experiments have also assisted me to have the things that no one has, my friend. It is your choice, if you do not want, Larry will guide you to the door," said the stranger, coming closer to Adrian.

"I've been striving to create this fluid for the past two months so that I can heal a girl who's struggling for life," he continued as he looked at the fluid.

"It is not difficult for me! To give blood, it is better to try than to leave it idle."

The Stranger glanced at the old man to bring the needle and the empty flacon to Adrian as he continued.

"I have heard a lot about you, that you are the author of many innovations and master such tricks that no one possesses."

"Well, if I was so clever, I wouldn't have come here today," Adrian said joking, as Larry approached Ad and asked to lift his hand so that he could puncture the finger and take the blood.

"Maybe not every meeting is a coincidence, so we had to meet and that it would have some sacrament, in it," the Stranger said mysteriously.

"If it can save the girl's life, then it hasn't been accidental," Adrian said pulling his hand.

"This is it!" said Larry, taking the flacon filled with blood.

"Give what our guest has come for, Larry," said the Stranger.

"I hope this is what I came for, otherwise I have nothing to lose," Ad said as he took the filled flacon.

"I have no habit of cheating, my friend. Believe me, this is more than you can imagine."

As they made their way out of the room, the lightning and the winds intensified as a result of which the window completely opened and the glass and accessories on the table fell, but the figures did not move.

"Here, sir!" Larry said, directing Adrian to the door. Ad watched the Stranger's calm and harmonious silhouette before the doors closed.

————— •••• —————

At Eisenstoff's house, everyone had already come to terms with the idea that the girl would not be cured anymore, and they were going to inject a special sedative to the girl so that she would no longer be tormented and suddenly there was a loud knock at the door, Hanna's father opened the door and Adrian was completely wet and out of breath outside.

"I have something that will help the girl to recover!" Said the boy as he entered.

"And what?" asked Block standing afar.

"In the beginning, we need to deprive the body of the poison, then inject this fluid."

"And how are you going to do it?" Block said quietly.

"At first I will cut…"

"That's unacceptable!" replied Hanna's father to the young man

"It's worse than death!"

"We had banned this young man from spreading his crazy ideas in an understandable language!" Block added.

"If he keeps insisting on what he is saying, we will kick him out of town tomorrow!"

"The girl has been in a fever for more than a month now, so what's better-to look and realize your own helplessness or to try to save her life, even though not with the tricks you imagined," the young doctor reversed, and the sound of the thunder faded Block's answer.

"Enough!" Said Hanna's father, and continued,

"Please leave my house," he concluded.

The night did not want to end, as if it were a clear day, something was heard and seen from everybody's house. After meeting with Eisenstoff the young doctor returned to his home near the central tower of the Dwinerd, deciding not to speak but to act. Adrian was standing in front of a mirror. His hair was shaggy, the smell of moisture was coming from the suit, enhancing his body, the fashionable tie was almost torn from the collar, and his face was covered in black spots.

"They'll be scared if they see me like this," Ad said in her mind. Approaching the sink, the young man washed himself long and patiently, completely changed his clothes, and only looked at the table in the basement of his lab. Hanna Eisenstoff was laying on a flat, spacious table. The severe fever had deprived the girl of almost all fat, and her skin was completely transparent, her veins, her muscles were clearly visible, and her ribs protruding like a monster's fingers trying to get out of her chest. Adrian lit the torches hanging from the basement walls, and a well-equipped laboratory was opened in front of him, with all the necessary containers, tools, and a desk. The laboratory was his own kingdom, though rejected by all.

"That is why this night is so long!" Adrian said so sure approaching the girl and Hanna, who had come to consciousness only for a moment during that period, realized that somebody had kidnapped her from home, carried her away in the rain, and that she did not remember how Adrian was lowering her to the basement, laying down on the table, making tools, and here again the windows open after the following lightening rumble, and the wind penetrating into the room, shutting all the curtains, as if unwilling to let the disease out of the girl's body, but everything calms down in the meantime and the curtains stand in harmony.

———— •••• ————

Recovering in the morning, Hanna saw only the amazed look of her parents and felt that the depressing weakness of her body of recent days was gone, and the news of the girl's recovery was quickly spread throughout the city. Everyone attributed Hanna's recovery to neighboring priest Frantz's persistent prayers, and the girl's dream of being kidnapped at night didn't impress anyone, and the family generally preferred to remain silent about the scars that appeared on Hanna's hands and chest.

CHAPTER III
The Bright Desert

••••

Oasis of Experts

Not far from the Dwinerd, the city of connoisseurs, in the southernmost part of Darwar, where the deserts lay, there was an area around which legends revolved. The area was completely covered with sand and dry winds, and only the bravest could enter that area as there were no vital facilities to live there, the sacrament of silence everywhere, and reflections of very bright light. It was said that a supernatural force was formed in that area, which knew neither time nor space, and the oasis of connoisseurs was situated there in the depth of the sand, where the strongest or the most advanced connoisseur could reach. The area was called by many names - the kingdom of light or a volcano of light or just light, as everything was bright and it was hard not to associate them with light. There was a huge abyss in the lap of the sand, in the middle of which was a cylindrical stone table with a wooden container filled with sand on it with traces of dried red liquid, that liquid was the blood of the people- the connoisseurs, that were coming there to fulfill their ideas.

The whole essence of that container was that if the connoisseur who was able to overcome the difficulties created by the desert and get there he would have to pour a small portion of his blood into that container and then say what he wanted to discover and the mighty power and mysterious light of the deserts would either have given him that idea, or simply nothing would have happened, and the connoisseur who had dared to reach it would be forever encased in the sand. In addition to rumors circulating about this area, that everything there was frightening and only death was awaiting those who would enter, there was another reality, that all was green in that area and it was the most beautiful place for people to rest, that light that was shining, there was a blink of justice and wisdom, and in time only good came from it, and intelligent connoisseurs were able to take advantage of that opportunity and had great opportunities to advance science for the benefit of people, but over the centuries people have misused this gift of nature, and have begun to realize their evil ideas through that power, and over the centuries, the light that once gave life to humans, was now taking it away.

There was a princess living in the bright desert, who was the only girl of that kingdom, whose name was Arishta. This region was known for its most beautiful leaders and with a family that had a milky body and dark brown eyes, there were legends about them and people from all kingdoms wanted to come and meet local girls. But wicked people who wanted to seize the supernatural power of that place, they destroyed whatever they saw and it vanished with all its beauty by attacking and Arishta was forever buried in those sands and they say, that her soul still existed and she lived in the deepest part of those sands and it was in harmony with the whole region, it could take the form of wind, sand, hurricane and preserve what was left there.

It was evening, the sun was almost over the horizon of the bright desert, and the sky was full of very dark and bright stars illuminating the desert, by which the absorbed sand seemed to be made of gold, and a man with a scepter in his hand was standing in the heart of the desert depressed and tired after a long way, untouched, untouched scepter in his hand, beneath which was the abyss - the oasis of the connoisseurs.

Only a few hundred steps were left to reach the container, but in that vast desert, every step seemed to be an eternity. The container was right in the middle of the abyss on a sand hill in

order to reach it you had to jump from a nearby stone pillar, in case of a bad bounce, all the past path would be eliminated in a moment and people would simply forget about that connoisseur, as it would be impossible to find him and no one would have known about him getting there.
Putting aside all that could be a burden and after using a few drops of water that were left, the connoisseur would get ready to jump.

"It will be very funny if I can't jump!" The scientist mumbled.
As he bounced, he could hardly reach the edge of the hill, and his hands clenched firmly, and his feet hanging over the path were hitting the hill while finding support in the air, and the sand particles were falling into the abyss.

"You can!" The connoisseur was screaming with great difficulty, in order to get the strength to overcome the hill and overcoming he shook his hands and body covered in dust, then he looked down into the abyss.

"I wasn't coming here to fall down!" and then he turned to the stone table on which the container was placed. In the distance, the sound of a storm was heard, which wasn't formulated yet. There were a lot of iron items on the table-coins, containers to drink water, that were completely dry of being in the laps of the sand, but there was also a strange iron knife on the table, the handle of which was adorned with unknown patterns, and as if it had not yet rusted and shone under the rays of the stars. Then he looked at the contents of the container, seeing the dried red-golden sand. Taking the knife, he knew what he had come for, and after crossing so many paths, he did not wish to waste his time, and looking up at the starry sky, he then whispered to the container.

"I give you my blood,
my essence, and please give
me what I came for!"

Keeping in mind the very idea, he stretched out his hand and pulled out the ring, which he put on the table, and carrying the knife on all the fingers, the blood slowly began to come out and he put his hand in that sandy container, and the sand completely absorbed the blood, and the connoisseur's hand became white and seemed as if it was not cut. After a moment of perfect silence, the connoisseur noticed as he looked stunned at his hand and then around him, he noticed that the sound of the storm coming from the abyss was getting stronger and closer to him, the connoisseur whirled around that table, and the sound of the storm grew louder, and the whirlwind of a sandstorm began from the edge of the hill that swallowed up the entire hilltop around which the table was placed, and in front of the connoisseur it was now only a hurricane and loud sound, which was reminiscent of a girl's scream, then the storm swallowed the connoisseur, and after that, the area was left alone on the table with the connoisseur's old ring.

CHAPTER IV
Revival

••••

Dwinerd

Adrian was walking through the endless plains of the desert and trying to escape the abyss of sand and each time walking as he was realizing that he had already survived, the sands, however, were starting to open again, creating large holes, from which Adrian again was escaping, and finally overcoming the following hole, Ad realized that he finally survived and he was walking on the plane sand towards the infinity, and suddenly the abyss began to form around him again, and he had to jump to avoid falling into the abyss around him, and just after the long jump, he woke up.

"Uh..." breathing deeply, Adrian opened his eyes and looked around fixing for a moment, that everything was fine, he woke up and went toward the sink.

"What a dream!" Ad was saying washing his face and taking a deep breath as he was washing his face again.

This morning Adrian had woken up earlier than usual and though he used to go down to his study- basement, this time he decided to climb the roof to enjoy a little fresh air of the new day. But the morning seemed strange to him as the light was shining brighter than usual, and his eyes were starting to hurt because of the reflection of the light. Everything seemed so bright and strange, as reflections intensified, Adrian decided to go down to the basement to his lab.

"I haven't slept well for sure! Dan was right," Ad was mumbling going down the stairs, as he continued,

"I need to work less and sleep more," reaching the basement and putting the following object of study on the desk, as he started to prepare the materials for the experiment and approaching toward the special stove, where he usually was warming up the liquids he had prepared. He decided to switch it, but before making the fire, he stopped for a moment and rubbed his eyes saying.

"If the light of the sun hurt my eyes, I think the fire will totally damage them!"

He switched the fire, trembling and noticing that nothing happened, he relaxed and boiled the liquid calmly, then he walked toward the window to open the curtains, but moved back, as the bright sunlight burnt his eyes again and he closed the window as he threw the newly made liquid out of his hand.

Adrian's assistant, Luna, who was a neighbor's daughter, despite her young age, was quite experienced and used to help Adrian in his experiments. Coming to the house for the following working day she noticed the voice of the barking dog and no one at home, so she decided to go down the basement quickly, where Adrian usually spent most of the day. As Luna went down the basement stairs, she noticed from above that there was no light in the basement and she quickened the footsteps reaching the study, as she noticed that all the windows were closed and not noticing Adrian she approached the window to open the curtain, but she heard a voice from behind.

"Do not open, Luna!" Grumbled Ad.

"Adrian?" Leaving the curtain, Luna turned around and didn't notice him, as she continued.

"Where are you?"

"Look to the right," Ad said, and Luna turned to look at Adrian in a corner covered in dark.

"What happened, why did you shrivel?"

"I don't even know how to explain it," trying to get up and approach Luna, Ad noticed the light shining from the window and went back to the dark corner again,

"You'd better find my friend Dan, please!" Luna was just silently following Ad's words attentively,

"He's in the center of the fair at this time of the day, as soon as you get there, ask people, and they'll tell you where he is," Adrian concluded.

"Ad..." Luna tried to talk to Adrian, but she realized that he needs help and Adrian covering his face with the scarf, heard Luna's departing footsteps.

Sarhat

Sarhat was not as old as Dwinerd but a newly created and was called a city of persecuted from Dwinerd and they were persecuted, as those connoisseurs were sent there, who behaved badly in Dwinerd and were sent there as a punishment. It almost constantly rained in Sarhat, and the weather was foggy, you would rarely see the clear sky full of sun rays, and the experiments of local connoisseurs who didn't have the proper equipment would pour all the bad effluent into nature, further degrading the atmosphere. The city was situated behind the upward mountain and that mountain had an equal power like God for inhabitants of Sarhat, as it was protecting them, even stronger than the fence. Over the years new generations had been formed in Sarhat and unwillingly were also in a condition of prosecuted, but people there were said to be kind despite how badly they were treated.

Valmar was leading Sarhat, who was the same age as Dargen and served to Dwinerd almost as long as Dargen, just because his views contradicted the ideas of Dwinerd he was sent to serve in Sarhat as a punishment and he was dismissed from all sorts of official positions.

"Where is our connoisseur!?" Valmar asked the advisor angrily, who was standing in front of him.

"The second one did not return either..." he was unable to continue as Valmar interrupted him almost shouting.

"But we had given him that boy's blood!" he said, rising and thinking a little.

"Everything had to work!"

"Unfortunately, but he also didn't come back," the advisor said the hopelessly.

"Don't you understand that I need this invention, otherwise I will not be able to fulfill my idea," Valmar said approaching the advisor more, as he continued,

"I now have what they have in their so-called University, but I have no more to put an end to their sordid and omniscient status!" looking up where the light was penetrating the room with so little light, he continued,

"That is why I need Ralph chandelier and for it to work!" Valmar said to the adviser standing just in front of him,

"And for that, I need that light."

"Mister, we already have the chandelier," the advisor said nearly trembling, as he continued.

"Our people managed to take it from Ralph's University."

"At least one good news for today!" Valmar said returning to his seat.

"We should continue looking for that light."

"Yes, sir! but we don't know who to send there," the adviser said.

"Nominate it to..." thinking for a moment and understanding who to send it to he said,

"To Alia."

City Fair

Luna went out to look for Dan without saying any odd word, as Adrian was generally more talkative, but this time he was so brief that she understood that everything was serious. Leaving the house, she immediately got on a horse that was nearby and rushed to the city fair. Luna was very clever and could quickly orientate and give quick solutions. Reaching the fair, she went to the most central part without hesitation, where mostly big crowds of people were gathering and she noticed a big amount of tall and sturdy people, who were approaching her, as she was shouting.

"In which part is Dan working?" as she continued.

"Adrian is looking for him!" But her gentle voice did not reach the crowd because of many people and because of indifference, somehow, she managed to get through the crowd to the small square, where there was a fountain in the middle and upon reaching that fountain, she sat down expecting to have a little rest. After looking back and forth, she saw that some mass of people gathered not far from the fountain, looking at a man who was showing tricks, and he went there, she saw a thin, tall guy, who could maneuver with hand movements and cheat people. Looking closely, Luna was able to guess his illusions and she was amazed at people's helplessness. Somebody shouted from a distance.

"Dan! do it again, please." Dan, the boy at once, came to Luna's mind, and she waited for the end of the event and approached the boy.

"Dan, did I understand right?" said the girl walking toward the boy.

"Yes, little girl, you want me to repeat the maneuver, but sorry, as more important things are waiting," said the boy, as he counted the collected money and put it in his pocket.

"No! Adrian sent me here to find you. He said that he needed you," said the girl turning around from the flow of many people.

"What has happened and why he sent you, the one who I don't know?" Dan replied indifferently as he walked forward.

"He teaches me and I am his assistant," somehow passing another flow of people Luna continued.

"This morning I went to his lab and I noticed him sitting in the corner on the ground and he told me to find you."

"Hmm..., that's weird, he usually sits on people's back, not on the ground," he paused for a moment and continued not looking to any side,

"So, something has happened," And Dan continued walking indifferently.

"Sir!" said Luna to Dan rudely, standing in front of the boy,

"If he didn't need you," And at that moment a line of horses passed by, muffling Luna's voice, and Dan just saw in front of him a girl who had been explaining things for a very long time, but he didn't hear her, and suddenly the flow of the horses was over, and Luna's word also ended, from which only the last word was heard.

"From behind," Dan said, looking at the girl's stubborn look for a long time.

"You look very stubborn! Only for that reason, one can believe you," And he noticed a large stream of people following the girl, approaching the girl's side, as he pulled Luna to the right, saved her from the collision and smiled in response.

———— •••• ————

Dan and Luna were in Adrian's lab, and Dan took the wooden horse figure on the wardrobe and said, playing with it in his hand.

"Probably it's because of not sleeping well. I told you to work less," Dan was saying to Adrian, who was sitting in his dark study, the scarf on him again.

"I don't know, Dan! But it's definitely not because of being tired. I have a strange feeling," Ad continued again, as he analyzed what had happened for a moment,

"Before that I had a dream about how I couldn't survive the pits of sand in the desert."

"Desert, holes?" for a moment Dan's look froze,

"Hmm…, I think I have heard such a thing," said Dan turning his look towards uncertainty.

"But I don't believe in such things, how can my dream be connected to all this?" Ad was saying sitting in the corner, and Luna was just following them.

"So, if you manage to cure the girl, we all know very well, how, it doesn't surprise you," said Dan refreshing his frozen look and activating, as he continued.

"And the dreams amaze you. What a strange person you are! And why such things happen to you especially?" Said Dan playing with the wooden figure in his hand again.

"You say that you've heard such things, what do you mean?" Ad asked.

"Well, you wouldn't like what I have heard," Dan said as he approached the window covered with dark curtains.

"Believe me! nothing can surprise me more than this, state,"Ad replied sharply.

"And I thought you were not naive," Dan said, standing by the curtains, as he continued,

"It is said that there is a legend about the Bright Desert."

"Bright desert?" Luna said quietly.

"Yes! about the bright desert," Dan turned around and continued,

"Do you know anything about it, little girl?"

"Not much. My parents used to talk about it a lot, they said we came here from there, because there was nothing but sand and aridity," Luna replied modestly.

"Yes, I knew that you were a clever girl, but there is something else, that very few know about it," Dan paused for a moment.

"The Oasis of Connoisseurs."

"I only know Oasis!" Ad laughed and continued,

"But I haven't heard about the Oasis of Connoisseurs."

"There is an Oasis of Connoisseurs in the Bright desert, where the omniscient would go and get the answers to their undetected discoveries." Dan said all this while slowly opening the curtain and very small ray of light penetrated and he noticed Adrian, who got immediately depressed of that light and he continued as he immediately closed the curtain,

"But while it sounds great, there is another side of it."

"And?" Ad asked after attentively following Dan's words.

"And..." Dan stopped for a moment, then he continued,

"Nobody returned from there yet!" Everybody froze and looked at each other and at that moment the voice of the merchant was heard outside,

"*Fresh Larms straight from the Southern sea*" Everybody came to senses as Dan continued again half opening the curtain and looking out and noticing Adrian's depressed look because of the light sun rays, then he continued,

"But I think we have nothing to do with it," and he said as he closed the curtain,

"Of course."

"And how can we know whether we have anything to do with it or not," Adrian said half standing.

"Well, I have a friend, far from the city, very far to the northern side, he's a priest, and he knows a lot more than I do, and he might be able to help you with that," Dan said.

"Us!" Luna added, as she also stood up.

"I don't believe in priests!" Adrian said as he pulled the scarf on himself again and went back.

"That's why we need to find him, to understand how much he can be helpful for us," Dan said mysteriously looking at Luna, as he continued,

"And that's why we need to begin the journey!"

Southern Guard

From a distance in the South, an armed man armed was coming on a horse in an iron helmet, which you would not see in these areas, he was coming from afar, who was holding a special iron sign, which was prepared by the king's order, and only special occasions, noticing that sign all the people, who obeyed the king of Darwar, were going toward that person. Otherwise, the punishment was inevitable. Reaching the southern entrance to the City of Connoisseurs-the Dwinerd, he was immediately let in and directed to the chief of the city guards.

"You have passed a long way to get here and you need some rest," the guardian said.

"Yes, sir! But my duty is, above all, and I will rest on the way. I have been directed to pass this to you," he gave the iron sign to the Guard.

"Welcome! Unfortunately, you can't stay long," said the Guardian, taking and examining it.

"The king highly appreciates the role of your city in this region and hopes that everything will be fine and there will be no need for interference." They looked at each other for a long time, so that they seemed to be talking, with the soldier's gaze, that only a person in service could understand, and then the man left the room.

CHAPTER V
The Armless Priest

....

Away from the city

The rays of the sun were increasingly drying up Adrian's face, causing holes that looked like traces of sand after the storm, and for that reason, he put a shawl so that no one would notice it, and he and Dan were on the road.

"You don't look so good brother!" told Dan to Adrian, who were in the locked dark cabin in backside of the riding carriage with a horse.

"Yes, so I will hardly get married in the near future," replied Ad, leaning in the corner and moving from one side to another from the horse-riding velocity.

"And not just get married!" asked Dan continuing,

"Do you know how much money I have given to this horse to get us to the place? That is why you have to get married and get rich."
For a moment Ad just looked at Dan without emotion and then they both started to laugh and at that moment the horse stopped abruptly and some voices were coming from outside and Dan confused and surprised, opened the window curtain and putting his head out screamed to the rider.

"What happened!? Why do we stop?"
The rider was not in his place and Dan could not see him, after a moment of silence the rider answered.

"Mr. a little girl is here!" and after a moment he continued screaming again.

"Where to!?…," Upon hearing footsteps, the cabin door opened and Luna entered from the outside very quickly and the rider followed her.

"Everything is normal!" Replied Dan, stopping the rider by the hand and continued,

"As I have said you are very stubborn, little girl."

"My name is Luna! and you'll be lost without me." Conveniently sitting in front of them, the girl continued talking.

"Then I brought a special substance, this will help him to alleviate wrinkles formed on his face."

"Let it stay," said Adrian, not letting Dan to express something and continued,

"Let's see what have you brought? " Luna handed over the medicine and they moved on.

Ralph's University

A regular meeting was held at the Ralph's University, where all five connoisseurs had gathered, and according to the regulation Dargen presided over that session.

"Greetings friends!" And looking at the Scholar sitting in front of him, Dargen continued.

"Begin Willmah, you've always put us on the right path!" Willmah was the most farsighted of all five connoisseurs, and many times he managed to surprise the Council.

"I have studied this issue and got acquainted with the available materials and I think that is connected with the Bright Desert and those lights are not accidental, just are manipulative. I think somebody is trying to use that oasis to their advantage." For a moment fixing that everyone was listening to him very carefully continued,

"And not a worthy person has not gone there yet."

"But how did they manage to get there?" asked Randolph.

"I don't know, but I think somebody is dictating them to go there and find something." Willmah replied calmly.

"But there was no news from that area for a long time and they say that this power of the Bright Desert does not work either and that power had already been sank along with the sands in the desert." Continued Vam.

"And where is Karma?" asked Dargen.

"We have no news from her since the morning," said Randolph distracting from the topic and continued,

"Although she knew that we should have a meeting today." Suddenly the door opened and Karma came in and everyone turned to her. Karma was a tall woman with long black hair. Quickly approaching the table, she raised her voice.

"I have bad news! Dear council," said Karma unable to cope with the breath.

"I hope that will justify your absence," continued Vam.

"Ralph's torch is lost, it's gone!" Karma said in confusion.

"How!?" asked Dargen.

"I don't know in the morning I was going to come to the session, but I decided to go to the library to get some extra materials and noticed an unusual silence.

Settling around the table, Karma continued,

"And I went into the storage room and noticed the absence of the torch there."

"And the guards?" asked Randolph angrily.

"We are senselessly wasting time." Dargen got angry and continued,

"We are still thinking and finding out, but the danger is far ahead of us and it acts very clearly and planned." Taking a moment to calm, she continued her speech again,

"Eventually we need to understand why they are doing all this to be able to stop it." Looking at Vam concluded Dargen.

"We must send a troop to Sarhat," said Willmah, and continued,

"And to arrest everyone!"

"We have no evidence that Sarhat is involved in all of this." Continued Vam.

"Vam is right, we have nothing," Dargen said. Willmah continued.

"Valmar has always dreamed of destroying Dwinerd and taking over Ralph's torch, so the city guards must be sent to Sarhat at least to conduct inspections on behalf of the University."

"Yes, we will," continued Dargen clarifying Willmah's words.

"And be sure to enhance the security of our archives in order do not miss even a hair from there."

"But why did they need Ralph's torch?" Randolph joined the conversation and noticed,

"Without light, no one needs it."

"That is the answer to all this," said Karma and continued,

"Those lights that are from the south are just for that torch, now they have the torch, and tomorrow they will have the light." Finished the speech hopelessly.

"It wasn't that hard to guess," said Willmah.

"Yes, but they should be hindered," countered Karma.

"How to hinder?" Staring at Dargen for a moment Vam continued,

"If there is someone who organizes secret meetings with them." Not turning his gaze from Dargen, Vam concluded and everyone was silent for a moment and looked at Dargen.

"What do you mean, Vam?" Dargen asked quietly.

"I was informed that one of the scholars had left the city and met with Valmar, but who I didn't know," said Vam.

"The next time before providing information like this, please speak based on facts!" Dargen grew angry and Vam just kept silent and looked at Dargen mysteriously and Dargen continued.

"Dear council, please be vigilant and very careful about the steps taken." Moreover, feeling that everyone was listening attentively, Dargen continued staring at Willmah.

"So, we'll send a group of City guards to Sarhat and find out what they have to do with all this." Taking his papers off the table, Dargen continued,

"We will understand from Sarhat's reaction how much they have to do with this, and now I consider the session closed."

The council was already preparing to disperse, and Dargen approached Vam as he prepared to leave and told him.

"At the end of the day come to me, please!"

Just nodding his head and following Dargen's departure, Vam also walked out of the room.

All the scholars had already returned to their workrooms, and on that day, there was a letter on everybody's table containing the same contents,

"Tonight, we gather in the secret room of the University."

——— •••• ———

Once again, dark clouds began to accumulate in the sky, and the horse-drawn carriage with Adrian and his friends was heading to the deep north.

"They say that he has no hands because he was once deprived of both hands for his quackery and sermons," said Dan, moving a small thing in his hand, much like a wooden horse.

"And we're going to him," Luna said frightened.

"They say we should be afraid of people who have everything and those people who are deprived of many things, even of their own hands, we should not be afraid of them since they have even more important circumstances for living and giving. Look at our friend." Adrian was leaning against the window curtain and trying to sleep.

"He is gradually losing a part of his body and I can say you'd be afraid of him." Looking at Luna for a moment, Dan continued.

"I don't think so!"

"But if he were good, he wouldn't be deprived of his hands," said Luna.

"Little girl, I'm not saying that he's good, I'm saying he can help us," replied Dan.

"The drug helped," said Luna looking at Adrian's face.

"Yeah, by the way, you look small, but there is a lot of persistence in you. So you have found me to help Adrian and now you found some weird drug that helped him, you stop the horse to help him again.

"Why, why does the little girl go north to help a man she doesn't know so well?" Inquired Dan.

"I don't know, he's just a good person." Keep smiling, she looked at soundly sleeping Adrian and continued.

"He teaches me things that I cannot learn anywhere and in the future, I want to become like him and help people." Turning to Dan, said Luna.

"But wherefrom the drug you gave him?" Dan asked again.

"My grandmother is from the Bright Desert and she has so many remedies, and she gave me that." The girl responded with a deep breath.

"What about your parents?"

"I don't remember them, my grandmother told me, when we moved from there to the city, they stayed there and then we had no more news about them." Suddenly the horse stopped and voices began to be heard from outside.

"Why are we stopping? " Asked Luna and continued,

"What happened?"

"I think we've reached the city border." Said Dan, pulling the window curtain and continued.

"Don't say anything!" And their door opened and the light came in from which forced Adrian to throw his shawl on himself and one of the border guards said.

"Introduce yourself, gentlemen!" Looking to the right and left, the border guard was examining.

"Sir! there is a little girl with us and I think her mother would not like it if someone told her that she was a gentleman." Roughly replied Dan and the border guard hearing the answer even more furiously tried to get in and countered.

"What's the purpose of your trip!?"

"Sir, do you see this bound man? He is sick!"

Hearing the expression " *is sick* " the border guard went back frightened and Dan continued.

"And we take him out of the city so that the disease doesn't spread on people." The border guard went back further and left the cart. Dan continued again,

"Don't be afraid you won't get infected do you see this drug?" Taking a small part from the girl's hand, he passed it to the border guard and continued,

"Apply on your hands and then wash." And Dan hasn't allowed the border guard to realize what was going on, continued.

"We were directed to the north by the Ralph's University to isolate the infected, and then they have to do tests to prevent the disease if it spreads." Speaking quickly, Dan panicked the border guard.

"Have a safe journey!" Taking the drug confused added the border guard.

"Thank you, sir!"

Dan instructed the horseman to move forward and shut the door. Voices were heard outside, and then they moved on.

"Have you always been able to do so?" asked Luna.

"What little girl?" Shaking his wooden stick, Dan asked with satisfaction.

"Easily cheat people." Looking at the wooden stick again.

"I do not cheat on them. I told them what they wanted to hear."

"But you have deceived that we are taking him into isolation." Said the girl.

"As long as we are here and Adrian enjoys his darkness," turning to Adrian for a moment, Dan continued,

"So, I said the truth."

Looking at each other for a long time they smiled and the horseman moved north.

Dargen was standing in front of the fireplace burning in darkness in his study, the light coming out of it was the only light source in the room and holding a tobacco pipe in his hand he was thinking about the content of the meeting with Valmar. He was worried about the expression of Adrian, which Valmar told him when was leaving. Suddenly there was a knock and Vam entered.

"Mr. Dargen," said Vam.

"Hello, Vam," Replied Dargen without turning around.

"Did you want to see me?" continued Vam approaching Dargen.

"They say he is a charlatan and he can make money by deceiving people." Smoking the tobacco pipe, Dargen continued,

"As well as he is very talented and has been able to help people and save lives many times."

"Hmm…, charlatan saves lives, it is very strange, and whom about are you talking Mr. Dargen?" Vam asked following the smoke coming out of Dargen's pipe.

"Adrian!" said Dargen turning to Vam.

"I met Valmar and he told me that name."

"Adrian? It looks like I have heard such a last name but I'm not aware, and that you met with Valmar I already know." Said the mysterious Vam and Dargen looked at him in amazement.

"Yes! Mr. Dargen, and not only you do know the secret ways to Sarhat," said Vam with a half-smile.

"You've always surprised me!" After a moment of silence, Dargen continued.

"Your brother as well."

"Yes, but compared to me now he is just in the area which is not liked by everyone," told Vam, removing smile from his face.

"And I'm not so stupid."

"Yes, you are more stupid!" Dargen sharply replied.

"If you think that I'm related to the disappearance of that torch."

"Hmm..., I didn't say such a thing."

"But you thought, your thoughts were higher than your voice," said Dargen, ironically.

"I don't know Mr. Dargen, but hiding from the council the meeting with Valmar and the name of Adrian, it raises questions among people." Looking at Dargen's thoughtful vision, Vam continued to speak.

"I think you need to explain at least."

"I don't need an explanation, Vam, and I advise you not to go where you can't find anything," said Dargen.

"In that case, may I get out?" Vam said coldly and ironically looking straight into Dargen's eyes and continued.

"Of course, if you do not need to speak." Dargen also carefully looked at Vam's ironic eyes, then said,

"You can go!" Vam turning his back over Dargen left the room.

Along the way, leaning against the corner Adrian has moved very little except for shaking right and left of horse riding and as he was on his way, he used to look at the side of the curtain slightly opened from where the light penetrated very little, but nevertheless, it came in and suddenly he noticed a reflection of a strange light and it seemed to him that a girl's voice was being heard and he was being told:

"Come back."

The light was getting brighter from that little corner until it finally exploded and he woke up and noticed Luna's unhappy face of a long way and Dan, who was enjoying the figure in his hand and looking at them again, closed his eyes.

"We've been on the road for several days and haven't rested, he needs some rest and we too," complained Luna and continued.

"He is completely exhausted we have to go out and find a shelter and after having rest there we will continue our journey."

"No! there is no time, every second counts," Dan replied Luna calmly, holding his nerves from the girl's moaning.
In response, Luna mumbled for a moment and started knocking the horseman to stop him.

"What are you doing?" Dan asked in amazement, partly getting out of his seat.

"I can't anymore, I'm going out!" the horse stopped and Luna approached the door.

"We'll rest for a while and go on again," said Dan, not letting Luna get out.

"We agreed!" Luna pulled her hand away and got off the horse. Outside was a damp forest, where the outlines of evaporated trees were visible on the horizon.

"Where do we?" Luna asked.

"We are in the North Forest, Miss," replied the horseman. Dan also followed Luna.

"We have to find accommodation until night so that we can stay the night according to the forecast it's going to rain," Dan noticed.

"Mr., we need two more days to overcome Forest," said the horseman.

"In that case, we should suffer," continued Dan.

"I don't have the strength to suffer either," Luna said sadly.

"In that case, you shouldn't come to the rescue your teacher, literally, little and much whining girl!"

"Yes! I'm small but smart, and now I want to rest for two days." As Dan and Luna argued the horseman disappeared behind them.

"Keep quiet for a minute," said Dan.

“I don't see our horseman.” Turning around confused, they did not notice that man around them, and Dan began to hear the sound of feet coming from afar, but he could not understand of which side.

"Luna go! And hide in the carriage quickly!" Dan ordered. Luna ran to the cart without hesitation, and getting inside saw Adrian asleep and shut the door, and there was silence outside. For a moment after the silence, the voices of feet became louder and Dan cried out.

"Close!" Then there was total silence. Luna's heart was beating very fast, she did not know what to do, and she thought it was all a dream and when she opened her eyes, everything would be fine in the meantime. People's footsteps sounds began to be heard behind the cart which were gradually getting stronger and suddenly the sounds lost again.

Luna hugged Adrian and with fear tears in her eyes said to him.

"Wake up Ad, please wake up!" After the complete silence, the cabin ceiling window opened instantly, but none appeared. Luna jumped up and closing her eyes, hugged Adrian even stronger, and then someone came in whom Luna didn't even notice and they put a scarf on his head and tied his legs. She could not confront them, and there was nothing left but to wait for the end. Thrown a cloth over the head Luna saw from the shadows that a group of people kidnapped them and took them in an unknown direction and the cart in which they were coming was set on fire, and Luna lost consciousness out of fear.

Dan was awakened by the droplets leaking on him from a wooden ceiling, and coming back after a few drops he finally noticed that they were in a damp wooden hut and next to him he saw the unconscious Luna, who was also bound.

"Luna!" Dan said in a low voice. Coming back Luna also noticed that the piece of cloth that was on her head was removed and Adrian was lying unconscious on the table, at a distance, without a shirt and Dan, who was next to her, was watching her and also was tied to a wooden pillar and raindrops from the ceiling continued to drop, humidifying the environment.

"Luna, how are you?" Dan said in a low voice.

"I don't know," Somehow holding back the tears continued,

"Where we are, you said that you know these areas." Dan didn't even manage to answer, when a group of people entered the room, among which was a man around whom everyone had gathered and that man looked at lying Adrian very carefully, then came and sat in front of both them, in the middle, clothes were thrown on him and his hands were not visible.

"Hmm…, you've come a long way from your home, and what are you doing here?" asked the man looking at Dan and Luna and continued.

"Friends and relatives are not waiting here, so you are lost."

"Yes, we are lost! "said Dan. And he was immediately shut up by one of the men standing, pouring cold water on his face.

"If you were lost you could go south!" the man got angry.

"But not north, I guess the false expressions at once."

"Sir," said Luna filling with tears, looking at Dan's wet face,

"We are looking for the Armless Priest to heal our friend."

"Your friend is already a corpse, nothing will save him."

"What have you done with him? " Luna said crying.

"We?" The stranger was surprised. Of course nothing, we are not murderers, life has already done with him what is necessary, and we will take what is left of him."

"Sir, we need help, this man who's lying there," looking at Adrian for a moment, Luna continued,

"He knows something that is the last prayer of all of us, and if we do not heal him, we are all destroyed."

"We are destroyed," everybody laughed at that phrase.

"Yes, we are destroyed!" Luna looked at the man angrily like fire and continued,

"The light coming from the south will destroy all of us." Dan looked at Luna mysteriously and Luna again continued,

"My parents have already been destroyed, and we are on our way to find the priest who will help heal our friend for fighting."

"And where from are your parents, girl?" The stranger asked quietly.

"From the south, the southernmost," Luna had already relaxed from the quiet response of the stranger.

"From the Bright desert, we have all fled from there and come to the city to escape evil, but the evil is closer than you can imagine."

"Little girl, I know what the evil is and I'm also aware of the Bright desert." The man said coming up closer to them.

"And do you know the name of the queen there?" Mysteriously asked the girl finishing his speech. Luna replied thinking for a moment,

"Yes! Arishta." The mysterious man nodded and they approached him and lowered his shawl. Dan and Luna noticed that he had no hands.

"Don't be afraid I'm not a Demon people, just evil people have decided to punish me and others like me and that's why we live here," Settling in his place, the man continued,

"I am the priest you want."

"We..." Unable to say anything, Dan was confronted by the priest.

"I think we did not let you speak, I am talking to the girl."

"We're here for our friend who dreamed of falling into the abyss of sand and can not be saved and after awakening, his eyes began to burn with the rays of the sun and we decided to find you for help." Luna was very clear and tender, only the person who had no heart could contradict or oppose her.

"But my girl helping her is already impossible, that evil has overflowed her whole body."

"If we lose him, we're all destroyed!" Again filling with tears and looking at Adrian's side Luna continued,

"I've seen it myself."

"Although," keeping silent for a moment the priest said,

"I have some substances that will relieve his pains, but I am unfortunately unable to heal."

"Thank you very much, sir, forgive my friend, he was lying to protect us, we haven't eaten or slept for almost two days. The priest, looking at the delicate features of the girl and struck by such a clear voice, could not restrain his smile and said.

"I will help you, my daughter, I've seen you are a good and honest person, I don't want to be the person who will ruin your perceptions of life, but next time if I see around such people, I will not spare you. And looking at Dan continued,

"But some investment will be required by you in return."

"Release their hands," ordered the priest to the assistant,

"The drug that will help relieve pain and heartburn is at the top of a nearby rock, unfortunately, I do not have hands to lift, and my friends are not generous like me, and I don't think you have enough strength to climb there," and everyone turned to Dan, and the priest told him.

"If you'll be saved and bring the plant, then we will heal your friend, if not then the world, as this little girl used to say, would be destroyed and we will join you very soon," Smiling, looking at Dan continued,

"Would you like to say something?" Everyone was looking at Dan carefully and he didn't say anything, but just shook his head.

"I knew that," said the priest.

"Let's go!"

The dark rainy night had already knocked on Darwar's sunset and all four connoisseurs, except Dargen, had gathered in the secret room about which was written in the letter, and it's possible to enter the secret room of the University with a special lighting torch.

"Dear scholars I know it's a difficult time, we all think of strange expressions of lights and Ralph's torch is lost, and we don't know why all this is happening, but I learned something that Dargen didn't tell us," said Vam, who had sent the letter to everyone.

"And what!?" said Randolph, and noticed that the window of the room was half-opened.

"I hope you have enough evidence to get us here and make such expressions!" added Willmah.

"Believe it more than," Vam said to Willmah and continuing pulled out a bottle from his pocket and handed it to Willmah and everyone turned to that bottle.

"This sign of our university is on this bottle," said Karma, looking attentively.

"Yes!" Vam said, and continued,

"This was found at a young man who had nothing to do with university, he is a wandering, self-appointed scientist who only knows how to steal."

"And where from do you know that guy?" Willmah asked.

"That is the main purpose of our discussion," Vam said very persuasively and continued.

"Dargen and Valmar have met."

"And except that they met, they talked about this guy, whose name Dargen has hidden from the council," said Vam very proud of himself.

"Hiding such meetings from the council, I think is a cause for concern."

"But for what should they meet and why the torch is necessary for Dargen?" said Karma not understanding anything.

"I don't know. I just know one thing that the boy whom our dear Dargen hides has gone north from the city." Becoming silent for a moment and coming up to the half-opened window he continued to speak.

"Maybe by going to Sarhat! And taking something with him, accidentally a torch and cheating on the guards and giving our university a name."

"You are very well informed, Vam," replied Willmah.

"Yes! Being well informed is my top priority as a scholar and I think we should find that guy and accuse Dargen for sharing secret information and concealing criminals."

"And how did you find out about the meeting and that guy in general?" Willmah asked.

"I was following Dargen that night, yes it was a part of my duties, if someone leaves the city, even Mr. Dargen," holdIng his breath for moment Vam continued again,

"But he told me about Adrian when he found out that I was aware of the meeting and by the way Dargen can prove what I have said." All the connoisseurs became thoughtful, and Vam pointed his hand toward the window and closed it.

"The old man needs to be awaken dear friends."

Everyone was standing in front of the rock, from whence the accumulated rainwater was pouring downward and waiting for the priest's instructions, the priest was standing in front of Dan.

"So dear..." waiting for a reply.

"Dan," said Dan partly trembling.

"Dan! That plant is right on top of the rock, you have two options for salvation, either you get there and lower the plant to save your friend, or you run away, with the tendency of never going down the rock again, as we all know very well how the rocks get wet in the rain and that going up there is probably easier than going down, for that I will help you." The priest instructed his assistant to hand him the worn cloth so that he could tie his hands, and Dan, looking at Luna's frightened and wet look, approached the cliff.

"So Dan today is the day of atonement for your sins, do not hesitate!" The priest shouted behind him and Dan approached the cliff and looked up and tried to put his foot on the first stone that came out and immediately slipped, the girl jumped up at that moment and shouted.

"Dan you can!"

He tied the cloth to his hands and began to climb the rock. The gushed out rain water poured into Dan's eyes and looking right and left in semi-darkness he could hardly find out the stones that came out, however, the power of fear of death pushed him further to overcome that rock and live. Reaching to the middle of the rock, in front of Dan the picture was already seen in two pieces, instead of one, and in his mind he was thinking how not to let the next stone out, so as not to fall down and by putting his foot to another stone, it fell down, and he could not keep himself and was holding on to another stone, and the water above immediately poured on his face, depriving him of reaching the end scene. The cloth tied on his hand was getting worn out, and the stones began to scrape his hands. Overcoming the rock somehow, he reached the top and saw the plant, and the girl screamed with joyfully.

"You did it, Dan!" And Luna's eyes were shining with happiness. Den looked at the plant and then down, seeing the outlines of the people in the rain, picked up the plant and looking down for a moment disappeared from the view of Luna and everyone.

"He probably went to pick up the plant," asked Luna the priest.

"I think he showed his face my daughter, and you also deceived me today about this guy that you want to save the country from the bright light, although you predictably said the right things but you just lied, I don't like lies and I didn't love either." And the girl was looking frightened at the priest, awaiting danger and frustrated by the rain.

"But don't be afraid I won't hurt you and I'll save your friend for your kind and positive nature, but it won't save you if you decide to lie again in the future," suddenly said the priest.

"I won't lie, I promise," said the girl in tears and continued.

"But the plant is up there, how can we take it?"

"The plant was a usual plant like other plants," calmly the priest answered, and Luna looked at the priest with surprise and did not understand what was going on. They went back to the hut where Adrian was lying and gathered around him. The priest asked the assistant to bring herbal medicines and cold water. After several hours of treatment, Luna tiredly closed her eyes and slept.

CHAPTER VI
Vision of The Death

....

Ralph's University

In the morning, Luna woke up from the recognizable voice and noticed Adrian sitting at a distance by the priest. Upon approaching them, he said nothing but simply smiled seeing Adrian's fresh face.

"You have to go back to the South," the priest said and continued,

"To Ralph's University and pick up the special Map that will show you the way to the Bright Desert, which will guide you to the Oasis of Connoisseur," the priest turned around and nodded to one of the assistants, who brought them a box.

"What is this?" Luna asked and the assistant handed the box to Adrian. Opening it he noticed a glass container the shape of which was rugged and looked like a diamond but composed of other forms, and there was a piece beneath on which handwork was very clearly visible. These two elements were in harmony as one single body.

"This container is made in the North and consists of special shapes. Water almost never heats up and never gets dry. However, there is simply no water there but just a medication. By a few drops on this piece, it can moisturize your wounds as soon as you notice that the wounds bother you. When this piece touches your body it will become a part of your body and will keep your identity in it. But it will not help you for a long time and you have to find that oasis before the water runs out, otherwise, the evil will befall you and you will be powerless against it. As you will not exist before getting there consider yourself to be resurrected and you must manage to find all your answers, otherwise you will be dispersed and will become a piece of sand."

For a moment, Adrian looked at that things attentively, closed it, placed it near him and said,

"Thank you very much! I owe you one."

"You will be thankful when you survive. And for now, let us continue our way while it is not getting dark," the priest stood up and Luna and Ad followed him.

"You haven't mentioned your name, sir!" Ad, noticed.

"Handless Priest, I think that is enough for knowing me," the priest smiled and answered peacefully.

They stood up and headed out in the direction where the horse was waiting for them, they sat down and moved towards the South.

It was Monday, an unusual Monday. There was an admission of young professionals to Ralph's University. They came from all over the world for admission and study. There was a celebration at the university, and at the same time a working whirl. The members welcomed them and guided for their future tasks, at the end, Dargen made his speech who used to make his speech at the end. Upstairs on the second floor Vam and Willmah were standing and discussing their daily routine and following the youth admission.

"What do you think? Why everyone is looking for that torch?" said Vam, looking mysteriously at Dargen, without turning to Willmah.

"I don't know, I know just one thing, this torch has never served for good in its history," leaning on the steel support which was in front of him,

"But I think this guy couldn’t do anything, he is too inexperienced to do such things, and I think they manipulate him."

"Everything is possible, my friend!" Turning to Willmah, Vam said and continued,

"Now are the bad times, you can expect anything from anyone for any penny."

"I can't disagree with you, but I have already sent a group of City Guards to Sarhat to do some survey," said Willmah, looking at Vam mysteriously.

"It was a bad idea from the beginning, Sarhat is an independent territory, and they have the right not to leave or not to obey at all," Vam said very confidently and turned to Dargen again.

"Well, I've already thought about it and that is why I have even sent a letter to the king for permission and they let me in by a special sign," Willmah said half-heartedly.

"A special sign?" Vam asked in surprise.

"Yes! the royal sign, if everything is okay, why Valmar should be afraid of the king anymore, he won't want war, it even sounds naïve." For a moment he noticed the troubled look of Vam who was looking down at the young connoisseurs acceptance ceremony, he continued,

"Something bothered you, my friend?."

"Worrying is my function, so it is much better, no more worries about that issue," replied Vam without any emotions.

"By the way… about our yesterday's meeting," Willmah gets closer and closer to Vam and says softly.

"Yes?" Vam asked.

"I just noticed the absence of a figure in the darkroom on the table," he approaches Vam and is about to touch him, then continues,

"One of them was missing."

"Hmm..., I didn't even notice, the employees have probably picked it up and forgotten about it," said Vam, looking down at Dargen as he approached the stage to say his word and continued not letting Willmah finish his speech and in a higher and rougher voice,

"Look! What an old man! At the first glance, he looks like a vulnerable man, but try to approach him and he will already be aware of your steps five steps ahead," turning to Willmah Vam continued to look into his eyes,

"But there is no man who has no weaknesses," Willmah accepted Vam's reply very calmly and left no answer, but left Vam to enjoying whatever he said, then he said very calmly:

"Dear connoisseur! You have forgotten that the figures were made of special wood, and only Ralph's heir could take it."

Willmah noticed the stunned and perplexed look of Vam and left.

———— •••• ————

The Sun was already setting, and only bright shades of light were outlined on the horizon, leaving the last rays of the day all along the Dwinerd, and Adrian and Luna were returning home.

"You said he had left," said Adrian, sitting on a horse, looking away at the Dwinerd's walls outlined by the sun's rays.

"Yeah! He has just left and gone," Adrian also looked at the city walls.

"Hmm…, it's weird!" he breathed for a moment and continued the horse's direction to the North gates of the city.

"Anyway, we're here now and everything's still fine."

"And how are we going to pass the walls? We were barely allowed to leave, and now we are going to enter."

"Don't worry! The gates are for guests, and we're not guests in this city." And by diverting the direction they went farther from the North gates to the South where the market entrance was located. And at a certain distance, there was a grassy section where there were located very small gates for importing goods to the city market where hardly one person could be fit unless he/she was not fat. By getting there they noticed that the entrance was almost closed due to not being unused and dirt accumulations.

"I hope you're not afraid of garbage! little girl." Adrian said, stopped the horse and the girl just looked at Ad in response. They got off the horse and approached that side and tried to clear the accumulated garbage, thereafter they noticed that the entrance was closed with grids.

"And that was your smartest decision," Luna said to Adrian.

"You're very impatient, of course, it is closed, who would open the grids of the city for the enemy to enter in?" He looked beyond the grids for a moment and continued,

"If not foolish peasant."

There was the dirtiest part of the city beyond the grids where abandoned and dispossessed persons lived, whose job was to clean the city's dirt, and who are indolent to get out of the city at night for discharging the garbage and opened the grids repeatedly so that the accumulated dirt could then be thrown out, and they discharge it in the morning. After a long wait, they noticed the approaching footsteps of people, and Adrian said.

"Luna, there would not be the second chance, are you ready!?" Luna nodded her head and when the grids were opened they threw themselves on that direction, the garbage was pouring down on them through the cylindrical pit, but they did not depressed, they went ahead into the pit and climbed upward by pressing on the narrow pit walls, but they didn't reach the top, they were left in the midst of the pit, as they heard the high sounds of the closing grids. They both looked down and understood that there was no way back, they turned back and saw a dirty, drunken man looking straight at them directly from the top of the pit. They were cramped in the pit and somehow managed to stop falling, their eyes were frozen and that man suddenly hiccupped and slept.

"Advantage for getting out from such a place!" Adrian joked, and they got up and came out of that hole. Going out, Adrian noticed people in strange armor, whose hoods were not matching with the city's coat of arms. Hiding in a corner and waiting for their departure, they went ahead.

———— •••• ————

Dargen was in his workroom waiting for his regular meeting. After drinking a glass of water from a glass cup in front of him, he began to examine a piece of paper held in his hand. He was reading sitting at his desk. The following was written,

"*Tonight, we are going to gather in the secret room of the University.*" There was no any emotion in his face, it seemed that he didn’t interested in what was written in that paper and what was going on behind him. He was looking ahead, deeper and he was very confident in what he was doing, and he did not doubt that everything would be as he imagined and by folding that letter he stood up to go to the direction of the fireplace burning in front of him. At that moment someone was knocking at the door and a young boy entered.

"Mr. Dargen," said the boy very softly.

"Yes!" said Dargen, as he folded the piece of paper and looked closely at the boy who walked in slowly.

"Mr. Dargen," repeated the boy very softly.

"I am hearing you, Dan!" said Dargen, and continued to direct the letter to the burning fireplace,

"Do you have any news for me?"

"Everything is done!" Dan said confidently, following Dargen's steps, and not daring to ask what he was doing and continued,

"They are already on the way, sir," following Dargen's movements again, who was already watching the letter burning in the fire.

"Very good, Dan!" Dargen turned his look from the fire to the boy and approached him. For a moment Dargen looked at the door to make sure that no one was following them,

"So, we're on the right track."

"Yes!" The boy said and Dargen walked out of the room and stood at the door.

"The problem is not over yet," Dargen looked straight into Dan's eyes and continued,

"They have a long way to go!" Dargen concluded his speech, the boy looked at Dargen and nodded his head. Dargen left and moved to the direction of the meeting room where the connoisseurs were gathered. In order to reach the meeting room, the corridor with long columns had to be crossed, at the end of which there were stairs. This corridor was the most famous in the whole university as it divided the workspaces of all the connoisseurs. Dargen walked calmly and noticed a strange silence. Even though everything seemed to be all right, something inside was disturbing him and he noticed for a moment that the corridor which can be easily overcome in a very short period of time seemed a lifetime. And finally reaching the staircase, Dargen noticed that he had already suffocated and that he needed a little rest to go up, but tiredness had swallowed him and he could not release the tension as if it had swallowed his whole body and, looking at the top of the staircase, he felt giddy, an unusual fever began to appear throughout his body, and, taking a few steps upwards, he just leaned on for a moment not to fall, and after a little rest he seemed to feel that the strange feelings were over. He tried to go up again, but he lost his consciousness and fell down.

——— •••• ———

In Dwinerd the lights coming out of all the huts conveyed a warm feeling to the city during the nights, and it seemed that they live together with the city. But tonight, the lights were inspiring a feeling of danger and fear. Adrian was in his lab with Luna, and they noticed that the lab was completely destroyed.

"I wonder who could do all this," Luna said in confusion.

"I don't know," Adrian said, trying to lift the things thrown on the ground and continued,

"But they were definitely looking for something!"

"And what?" asked Luna and Adrian, taking a figure out of his pocket, sat down around the table and continued,

"I think this," he finished his speech and put the figure on the table. The figure was very small, and looking at it you could understand that it was more like a bottle than just a regular wooden figure, and it was clear that there had been some content in it at some time because it had worn out holes, which were not subject to geometric explanation. It was obvious that something had come out of it.

"What is it?" Luna asked, looking at the figure very carefully.

"Just a figure! I don't know," said Adrian. And noticing Luna's frozen look at that little figure, he continued,

"Well, I think we'll still have time to think about that, but for now we have to act," and taking the figure back from the table, he kept it again.

"And how are you going to get that map?" Luna asked, diverging from the figure.

"Honestly, I don't know," Ad said, standing up from the table and walking toward the window from where they could see the tops of the University Tower from afar.
He just looked to that direction for a moment then continued,

"I will go there and tell everything that has happened to me and hopefully there will be good people to help me," and then Adrian turned to Luna and said,

"And you," for a moment, he took a breath and got closer to Luna and continued,

"Return home and pick up the most important things you can take, I'll wait for you here, just hurry up!" He looked behind Luna who was leaving, then Adrian quickly prepared a letter without wasting time, where the following was written.

"A little girl, who was able to be with me at the beginning of all my trouble and not quit, thank you very much and I think I have a lot to learn from you, we will see when the sun is not so painful, your Adrian." Writing this, Ad put it on the table and went out.

———— •••• ————

All the Connoisseurs had gathered around Dargen's immovable body, who had been taken to the University's combination room, he was lying down and they were unaware of what had happened. They silently watched to him who could hardly breathe. His body had been absorbed with the cold blue, and that color had become so intense that it seemed as if somebody had painted.

"All this only proves that Valmar is guilty and he must be destroyed!" said Willmah angrily, looking at Vam, and Vam was just standing in the corner silently. Willmah continues,

"But Valmar could not take such a step alone, Vam is also guilty in all these!" Willmah looked very attentively into Vam's eyes and continued,

"The continuation of his traitorous brother!"

"Vam was the one who served in the board for the longest time," Karma joint the conversation.

"And before blaming him, it would be better to find some arguments," said Karma also looking at Vam's who was just looking in one direction, but his mind was floating elsewhere.

"I will find the arguments!" Willmah said very calmly. And Randolph followed quietly the intense discussion of all the Connoisseurs, and when he realized that the time had come, he said.

"Dear Board," Randolph joint the discussion as well,

"I think we are not helping Mr. Dargen while we are here looking for guilt." He looked at Dargen's peaceful body and continued.

"We need a new leader, at least temporarily, to be able to understand everything," Randolph finished his speech.

"The election of a new leader is unacceptable!" Willmah abruptly replied and continued,

"After Dargen's death, the highest official subordinate to him should be appointed to the manager's position."

"Willmah, of course, I share your emotions and we all do understand very well that you should be holding that position, but at this difficult time we need to unite and if we all say things like this we will not get a positive results. Dargen has not been removed from his position and thank God he has not died and I think we just need a temporary leader before he can recover."

"And how should we choose a leader if Dargen was holding his position until his death. And to elect a new leader we have to organize meetings and set up a considerable procedure, in general," said Willmah.

"We will vote in accordance with the University's old traditions," Randolph said calmly and full of thoughts, and everyone was waiting for Randolph to continue his speech,

"In the old law of the University, in special cases, there is a choice when the

Connoisseurs and the Members make selections using special medals.

"But the old man will not be able to prepare such medals in such a short period of time," said Willmah.

"I think we all underestimate the potential of the old man," Randolph chuckled. Willmah was just standing in his place, he was angry, he looked at Vam and noticed his unconscious look, he continued.

"So, voting! But if the old man did not manage to properly prepare the items, I will not wait anymore and will take my steps," he just looked at Vam for a while.

"And of course, we will understand what actually happened to Dargen."

Vam and Valmar met each other at the biggest mountain of Sarhat where the whole city panorama was visible.

"You told that Dargen has lost his consciousness," Valmar asked profusely, walking around Vam and noticing a flower on the mountain that opened its leaves only at that mountain.

"You're guilty in all these things!" Vam said angrily. He followed Valmar who was examining the flower very carefully and continued.

"I could almost bring the attention of the board to my side without any incident and they would give me the status of leader by themselves, and now everyone disputes that I am guilty of that," said Vam getting closer to Valmar and again continues.

"You have been hasty, brother!"

"Hmm..., but there is a point here," Valmar said quietly while examining the flower and without tearing it.

"And what can justify you? Willmah had already sent a group of city guards to come here," Vam joins the flower scene of Valmar, then continues, this time more calmly,

"And after all these, thing he will send a royal army, you know, and you will be deprived of Sarhat, to say nothing of the torchlight, the University," and he noticed Valmar whose eyes turned from the flower to him and again told very softly.

"You have been hasty as usual, brother!"

"Well, the point is that I haven't poisoned anyone, my friend." Valmar replied half-heartedly.

"Someone has manipulated us, whereas we thought that we manipulated all of them."

"How come you didn't poison Dargen?" Vam asked in surprise.

"Who then did that?"

"Sure, I am not that person, I haven't poisoned, that's not my style, I like to act." Valmar looked at Vam.

"Like you! Brother, maybe cheating or distracting, but not poisoning, he was certainly not worthy of such death."

"He's not dead yet, he breathes, but given her age, the poisoning will definitely not result in a good outcome, but who has poisoned then?" asked Vam in confusion.

"I'm not a diviner, my brother, I'm just a man who wants to take over all these and you will help me, maybe his poisoning is advantageous for us, and we will more easily take over Dwinerd."

"Valmar! You are naive, the torchlight is not there yet, and Adrian's blood did not benefit us, but on the contrary it helped him move South, and we do not know what to expect there." For a moment Vam sighed and fell into thoughts again. with a frozen look on the city scene, he continue.

"Then Willmah told me something," for a moment Vam fell into his thoughts.

"And what did he say?" Valmar asked very quietly.

"He said there was no figure."

"What figure is he talking about, Vam?" Valmar asked anxiously again.

"The figure Ralph is missing!"

CHAPTERVII
The Leader

....

Dwinerd

This morning was very quiet and along with that, strong winds were noticed. The election of a Ralph's University Leader in Dwinerd should take place and flags were flown across the city to symbolize the importance of the day. The walls stretched from the south to the north of the city, with flags fluttering proudly from the wind. But one of those flags, unable to withstand the force of the wind, slipped from its position and fell on one of those walls, along the length of which armed men by a long column of were walking who were led by a man from the look of which you could understand that he himself was to head that column. As he approached that flag he saw the flag on the ground. For a moment, he looked intently at the emblem depicted on the flag, which had been glittering for several years in one of the most proudest of Darwar. He rubbed it and walked ahead.

"The whole crew is ready!" said the man in the iron helmet, who was in the Dwinerd guard room.

"We'll go when the order is given!" the Guardian leader replied, and went out of the room, and by the force of the wind, his hat dropped down from the walls to the side of Mount Sarhat. And he glanced at the mountain for a moment and then noticed a group of men who could hardly fit in the corridor located in the long walls. After a few steps, he just checked these people and noticed the flag lying on the ground. And as he approached that piece of the flag was already shattered, and the pride that was once existing in that flag was lost by now. He lifted and shook it and tried to fix it at its place. However, the wind was so strong that he could not do his job easily. He somehow managed to fix the flag in his place and then proudly went back to the room.

----- •••• -----

There should take place the selection of the head of the Board in the Ralph's University and all ten members and connoisseurs had come together to prepare for the vote. According to the University Rules, Willmah had the right to speak after Dargen's speech. Willmah had the highest title after Dargen.

"Hello, dear Members and Board! Today we have gathered here for a reason, as our very beloved Mr. Dargen is in very sick and cannot handle his position and we hope he will recover soon and be able to continue his work. But before that, we have to choose the leader for our University." And looking at the old man coming from afar who had already come to the meeting room by a special cart, Willmah continued.

"I consider the voting open!" According to the tradition, the voting should be transparent and everyone could see who has voted and whom has voted. And for that reason in the middle of the large room nominal supports for torches were located for the Connoisseurs. The torches made specially shall be approached and placed on those supports. All the participants had their own numbered medals to throw in one of the nominal torches whom would they prefer. And then an old man who was responsible for preparing special items for the university brought the torches. And he approached the cart very slowly, by a special cart, and placed the torches in their places and then burned them. The torches were burning with very low intensity, but with the medal, the fire started to intensify. At the end, when the selection was made, the owner of the brightest torch approached took it and said his words.

"The Members will vote first," And looking at them, Willmah continued,

"Please, you can come and throw your medals in a torch you prefer." After Willmah's words, the Members began to approach and throw their medals at the torches.

"Look at that old man," said Randolph, who stood by Karma.

"He has been making these things for centuries and has never been late," said Randolph half-heartedly.

"I think if I were him, then I would always be late!" Karma joked and continued looking at Willmah and Vam who were standing in the distance and just didn't notice each other.

"Do you think it was the right decision that we didn't concur Willmah and decided to make a choice," Karma said.

"Well, Mr. Dargen left us in very doubtful conditions and has gone for rest," and walked to Karma's side for a while and continued,

"And to pass the position just without voting, I think it was wrong!" Randolph concluded. Member voting was already coming to an end, and the torches of Vam and Willmah were burning evenly. And after the last members' medals, it was clear that Vam and Willmah had already gathered equal votes and the final medals were still held by the Connoisseurs. But as the votes were equal Willmah again made his speech.

"Dear Members and Connoisseurs! Thank you for your participation." Willmah looked at the side of the torches.

"Because the torch intensity is equal between for the two Connoisseurs, they must pass to close voting and decide who of them will become the leader. Thank you for your vote and participation, and so I consider the first round of voting to be completed, at the end of the day I will publish the Leader's name." Willmah ended his speech in a hurry and turned his look at the Connoisseurs. They approached him they went to the discussion room which was located right in the voting room.

———— •••• ————

The Sun was just setting, and Adrian had already reached the front of Ralph's University and was about to enter. Approaching the gates he didn't notice anyone, and after a few steps, the guards met him.

"Where are you going!?" there were two guards, but Adrian didn't notice which one was asking as they both were wearing helmets and their faces could not be seen.

"I must meet Mr. Dargen!" said Ad naively, hoping that they would concur him.

"And was Mr. Dargen aware of that meeting?" asked again one of them.

"Hmm…, no, but when he finds outs why I came here I think he'll want to talk." He answered, confused, not understanding who he was talking with.

"There is a ceremony at the University now, and we are ordered not to let anyone in!" said one of the guards behind the grids, and they just left without much word or answer. Adrian revolved at his place, decides not to give up and enter surreptitiously. He waited for the guard's shift in the corner. He runs to the grids and quickly enters overcoming some barriers. But one of the guards notices him and shouts,

"Stop!" Running long behind him, the guards lose Ad and Adrian manages to reach the back door and hide from the guards.

"There seems to be no one here," Adrian gasps in deep breaths. He goes ahead and as he goes up to the next grids his foot slips, he falls down and closes his eyes for a moment. Then he opened his eyes and notices the guards standing in front of him and looking at him. They lifted him angrily and twisting his wings, they guide them forward.

"I've never spoken to two people simultaneously," joked Ad and continued,

"My name is Adrian, and I have to meet with Mr. Dargen." The guards didn’t pay any attention to Adrian’s words, they tied his head to with a cloth and took him to University prison.

Connoisseurs gathered in a special room, trying to figure out who should become the interim leader of the University.

"And what are you going to say now, Randolph?" asked Willmah very calmly.

"Well, the choice is just to understand who should be the right person to lead this University."

"At your initiative, we are in a worse situation now, and this traitor was about to..." Willmah continued, looking at Vam,

"Become our leader!" when Vam tried to express something, Karma rather responded first.

"Willmah! Vam could be an as good leader as you and your confident accusations are groundless and cause us not to choose you."

"And I don't need that position," Willmah continued, looking carefully at Karma's face,

"I can concede my place Vam, it makes no difference to me. I am concerned about the consequences of what will happen to our university and the city in general if we have such a leader."

"Never mind, Willmah! If I am selected, I think that I will manage better than you!" Vam responded sharply.

"Vam has the longest experience in serving this University, and it's not worth any friendship. If we should only choose a leader who has a higher title and put aside his years of service and dedication to this University, I think it is not fair and that's why I vote in favor of Vam," Said Karma and stood next to Vam.

"Hmm..., it's your right, Karma! Just when you regret about your choice," he continued, sniggering.

"And not only the choice for selecting the leader, please do not tell me anything! I will do whatever I should do in that issue and will start right from discovering the poisoning matter of Dargen" said Willmah, looking at Randolph.

"And what would you like to say, Randolph?"

Randolph thought a bit then looked at Willmah.

"Yes, Karma is right, sorry Willmah! I respect your dedication and concerns in general, but all this time Vam has been more alert and neutral and I think the choice should go to Vam, I will also vote for Vam."

"Fools, the fools like you have been given it the title of a connoisseur by the University," said Willmah laughing.

"Willmah, by insulting us you are pushing us further away from you," Vam said.

"Hmm..., and by hiding your secrets. You insult not only us, but all the people gathered outside," Willmah said.

"I think our choice was very clear, Willmah," Karma said, looking at Randolph and continued,

"The University leader will be Vam for a while before Dargen heals."

And Randolph simply nodded his head showing the approval of the words of Karma.

"Hmm…, I will gladly accept the fact that Mr. Vam is now the leader, and will leave this room because my work is too much in comparison to you!" and Willmah said again, trying to leave the room.

"I forgot to say… to the interim leader," And looking at all the connoisseurs gathered there, Willmah left the room.

Adrian was tied with chains. He was trying to see where he was under the cloth put on his head. He only noticed the sunlight coming in through the small grids and illuminated the wet and old and damaged wall in front of him, which was reflecting the rays on him. Suddenly, noises were heard behind the prison door, and the iron door opened. A man came in and walked towards him, Adrian only heard the sound of footsteps walking from afar and the sound of the door's closing. And suddenly there was silence, and he felt that there was no longer any reflection of the accumulated light in front of him. Instead of it, the silhouette of a man was noticed.

"It is good when the sun goes down!" said the man.

Ad recognized that voice, but he did not dare to speak out but noticed that they had pulled the cloth on his head. Adrian nodded his eyes for a moment, looked closely at the man and said,

"Dan!?"

"Yes!" The boy answered, throwing the cloth to the corner.

"But you...," he continued thinking for a moment,

"What are you doing here?"

"I'm working here brother," Dan said trying to release Adrian.

"How, but you are a magician, what are you doing in the University?"

"No, my friend, everything is not too easy. I serve on the Board of Connoisseurs and personally Dargen. And I have bad news for you, the whole city is looking for you, and you have to be banished for stealing the torch and concurring Valmar," Dan responded to Ad.

"What are you talking about?" he looked at his hands twisted by the chain for a moment.

"I know there is no such thing, but the wicked have done everything to make it look like that. Vam, who was a member of the Board of Connoisseurs here, now runs the University and you were manipulated, my friend."

"I will prove that it is not true!"

"Until you prove the sun will surely swallow you up and burn you, that's why I'll help you."

"I don't understand anything, Dan!"

"You don't have to understand much. Time will put everything in place and you will understand. And now if you want to be saved then you must not stray from your path."

"How can I not stray? I need the map so that I can find that area, and I could take it only with the help of Dargen."

"You may probably have forgotten what I told you," Dan continued, pulling a round device from his pocket.

"What is this?" Asked Ad, surprised.

"This is the map you need. You will go to the South and believe me, you will understand how to use it."

Adrian took the strange device, looked around and joked,

"Hmm…, the maps I imagine look different," and continued to put it in his pocket.

"Luna told me you had just left."

"My stay was not so important, it was all done and you came to the priest. As I see the burns softened." Adrian was not able to finish his words when two very loud rumblings were heard behind the door.

"Let's go! We have to hurry." Dan said, and they got out of the prison and threw clothes on Ad's head again.

"Believe me!" Dan said, and they emerged, and Adrian noticed that he was being led to the small boat heading for the ship, sitting in which Adrian sat. Dan approached Adrian's ear and said.

"You shall move the figure toward the light!" Then he heard the leaving footsteps of Dan and noticed that he was positioned as a luggage in that ship and after a while, he felt that he was transported via water to somewhere, but couldn't understand where exactly. Suddenly the ship stopped and started to go up. When they reached the destination Adrian was again taken out of the ship like luggage and help him to stand up. Ad did not understand what was going on, many things were going on in his mind, but inside he felt that everything was going to be ok and he suddenly heard a voice.

"Once you reach the nearest southern port you can get down!" Said a man with low tempo, who pulled the cloth off of Ad's head very indifferently, turned around and looked at Adrian's eyes and left. Adrian noticed for a moment that they were on board and approached the edge of the ship and noticed that they had already moved. After regaining consciousness Adrian noticed that they were on ship, he approached the edge of the ship and noticed that they had already moved. Adrian just tried to relax before embarking on new adventures, and, looking deep into the horizon, he noticed a group of armed men who were going to Sarhat Mountain as well. But the thought that they were in a moving ship gave him a little rest and when he looked beyond the waves of the sea, he saw a fluttering flag trying to keep up with the last fluctuations in the water, but after fierce fighting the flag wrecked.

CHAPTER VIII
In The Embrace of Desert

••••

New Horizon

Adrian had been riding to the desert for several days and had been completely exhausted, his only thought was to have a rest and drink a few sips of water. Finally reaching the new horizon of the desert, Adrian saw a hut in the distance that had almost dried up and burned from the sun, he looked at the quantity of water and noticed that it was almost over, saving the drops he drank a few sips and when approaching the hut got off the horse.

"Our journey was over, my friend! I will only cause you trouble." Leaving the horse he approached the threshold of the hut and noticed no one there, only dried wooden things for years, and strange cleanliness, even the sound of a storm that muffled his ears in the desert unwittingly, but before he drew closer to the hut, the strange dryness on his hands and his sickness began to appear. He pulled out the piece and the water bottle, which had given him the priest, and wetting it a little, wiped his hands, his body was absorbed with a strange cold in that hot weather for a moment and he saw that the dryness of his hands disappeared. The piece with which he touched his hands, it had accepted the trace on his hand as if it had been mapped out, and, throwing those items entered the hut. There he noticed many items, whose dust seemed to be fresh and the sediment of time had not yet come to fruition. Apart from the obsolete items, there were obviously fresh traces, the wooden floor was very clean, which seemed to show the way, with which they had managed to walk many times before. Adrian following through the clear traces of the floor, he reached the middle of the room, where he noticed that the dust was coming out of his weight, outlining a hidden door. Looking at his sides, he noticed a table with kitchen utensils that had rusted over time, and, taking a knife from the table, he shook it to clean the rust a little. Then he approached the knife to the gap, which was between the floor, the rust pressed firmly on the knife, and Adrian was able to raise the door. Opening the door, he noticed a basement, and when he came down, he felt a very strong smell of moisture. Going ahead, he saw a huge quantity of water containers, his eyes shone, he just froze for a moment, but as he approached one of the containers, he was hit very hard and he lost consciousness.

——— •••• ———

The royal group had been in Sarhat for several days and had been able to block the nearby forests that were under Sarhat's control. Since Valmar had opposed the royal sign, the royalists had declared war on him, but the forests of Sarhat were not so easy to occupy and the heart of the city was at the back of the mountain, but to capture it they needed special material that would destroy and detonate the mountain and they would manage to enter there. The material was under the control of the University, and for obtaining it, the leader of Ralph's University, Vam, had to give his agreement. That is why, a huge crowd of people, who had escaped from Sarhat had gathered at the northern gates of Dwinerd. They were escaping from there and trying to find refuge in Dwinerd to avoid from the massacre.

"Vam, Dwinerd has not been so vulnerable yet, the population of Sarhat is fleeing here and harming the local population," Karma told Vam, who were in Vam's workplace.

"But we can't just destroy them or not to let them enter," said Vam, looking at the city, which was visible from the window of his workplace, and he continued,

"They are also people, just they have appeared other side of the gates", turning to Karma he again continued,

"Bad management of Valmar should not be the result of their slaughter."

"We must not let them get in our lands," said Karma, approaching closer to Vam and softening his voice, continued,

"Besides bad management Valmar poisoned Dargen, it was villain by side of him, and on the contrary, instead of persecuting him, Dargen gave territory to build his world and having what he has, he also wants to take possession of all this," holding Vam's hand, Karma continued,

"Dargen would not let him go in time, but send in persecution."

Vam turning back to the window and with a small breath he responded,

"Valmar is not guilty for poisoning Dargen."

"And how do you ensure, that it is true?" Karma was surprised.

"I just feel like he wasn't that stupid to do that."

"The royal forces have been there for a few days, and they are gradually weakening Valmar's position, and soon Sarhat will no longer exist," Karma said slightly raising the tone of voice behind Vam, who was just looking at the city.

"Yes! Willmah did that, he managed to take his revenge on Sarhat," said Vam with calm thoughts.

"Willmah is protecting Dwinerd, and what about you, Vam?" approaching Vam and stood beside him, Karma continued.

"Please choose your path!"

——— •••• ———

Adrian dreamed, where the desert started from horizon to horizon and all was light in the calm sky, as the light was going brighter eliminating outlined boundaries in the horizon and seemed there was a sound, a beautiful sound that grew louder than ever. That voice gave him an unusual warmth and stillness and he listens again,

"Come back."

Adrian quickly opened his eyes, noticed that he had been tied to the tree not far from the hut, and noticed a man, who was preparing something around him. Long waiting for an explanation by them, as why they had brought him there, Adrian exclaimed.

"Hey, you!" cried Adrian.

"Why have you tied me!?"

He looked at his distant water bowl with its stuff thrown to the ground.

"You don't want to answer your prisoner?"

That stranger had thrown a strange cloth on him, which was mingling with the sand of the desert, and approaching Adrian, the latter could not see the stranger's face, because his face was closed with a piece.

"What a mysterious people, all with closed faces, and why, who will answer?" Adrian groaned.

"Slow!" said the stranger, closing his mouth.

"Why should I be silent? I will be dry soon."

"Slow!" said the stranger, shouting again, closed Adrian's face with his hand.

"Hmm…, these are very delicate hands, I think I have been kidnapped by a girl," Adrian said with a smile.

"You have not been kidnapped, you have been saved, stupid!" the girl continued moving Adrian to the other side.

"I've been waiting for this for a few days, and you've come and spoiled everything,

I couldn't kill you, that's why I had to save you."

"From what did you save?"

In the distant at dark night, a storm began, and there was a sound of a strange shriek as if someone was crying, then they noticed footprints, but they saw no one.

"Silent!" said the girl, and approaching Adrian was hidden beside him and threw his clothes on Adrian too. Underneath the cloth were some strange animal sketches that you did not understand they were humans or animals that were slowly approaching the hut and creating a storm around them. As the whole storm swallowed the hut, the voices kept silent, and the sky became clear and the stars began to appear in the darkness. It was an incomprehensible simplicity, where they stood motionless under the tree, and Adrian whispered.

"What are they looking for and who are they?" The girl, comfortably accommodated and irritated by Adrian's questions, simply shook her head.

"You have arrested me, but neither you have not killed me, nor haven't left me there to be captured by those obscure creatures, nor now you are not talking to me."

"At least say something to make me realize I'm here, otherwise I'll go crazy and scream at those animals at least I will talk to them."

"Stupid, keep silent if they notice us, believe me, you won't speak anymore."

"And how do I know if I haven't spoken to them?"

"You want to talk, go!"

"But how? My hands are tied to the tree," Adrian made a joke again, and he continued to grow a little more serious.

"And more seriously what animals are there?"

"They are not animals, they were humans before, but now they just live here and dry everything, whatever they see, and I had barely found any water reserves and I was going to cheat them and at least I could take a little water, but you came and spoil everything."

"You could have not tied me here, just leave me somewhere to dry."

"Believe me, they would notice you, and I wouldn't be better afterwards."

"So, I am just a circumstance that cannot be thrown away, cannot be kept, I am just an obstacle."

"A lot of talk is an obstacle!"

"But I haven't spoken to anyone for a couple of days, but now I have the opportunity,"

Unable to continue, the girl tried to close her mouth with her hand, and Adrian bit it.

"Idiot!" the girl said and stroked her face with her other hand.

"Ah!" Adrian screamed and the hurricane started to get stronger at the hut.

"You are really fool, I had better to kill you, and now we will be both victims."

"Well, now if everything goes wrong there is a way that we can be saved."

"Yeah, they kill me early so I won't even listen you."

"I'm serious," said Adrian very definitely.

"There is one way." The girl said with a small breath and continued.

"Escape!"

"And how can we do that?"

"If we run away, we will be without water and God knows when there will be such a chance to find water."

"But now, whether we want or not, we will not be able to take that water," Adrian replied.

"You are mistaken, I have set a trap for them, when they fall in it, they will not be able to get out, and I will manage to take the water and run away.

"Ah, I could fall into that trap that is why you saved me."

"Either you will be silent or I will just leave and you will stay here with them, I hope you will not be deprived of the opportunity to speak," the girl said nervously.

"I'll help you get that water!" said Adrian.

"It's already late, there is still storm, so they are there and the trap hasn't been worked."

"I'll go and check!"

"You're actually a fool besides the talker," said the girl, looking closely at Adrian.

"You saved me, and now I will save us, as we stay without water, there will surely be nothing left for us in a few days," Looking at his hands that were wrinkled Adrian continued.

"I will go there, and if everything goes bad, you will be aware of it and will run away."

"You are so stubborn!" the girl surprised.

"Sooner or later I have to dry in this desert, at least I will have done something important in this life," said Adrian in half-smile.

"That is to say, you will dry," the girl continued without understanding anything.

"It's been a long time to explain, now I'm going to check, don't you want to leave my hands?" Adrian asked shaking tied hands.

"You're really stupid!"

"Yes."

Moreover, following how the girl tries to release herself again, Adrian added.

"And there is one thing I need to know if they are suddenly there."

"Yeah, run away!"

"Well," the girl released her hands, and looked carefully at Adrian's hands, on which there were dry traces.

"Well, if you notice that everything goes bad, run away, they will focus on me and you will have time.

“'Silly!", said the girl in harmony, but with a strange hope that everything would be fine.

"So, let's go drink water!" Adrian said with a smile, and slowly went to the hut. Reaching the hut, he was connected to the storm, and approached the entrance. From there was listening a screeching coming from a distance, and he noticed the grains of sand coming out of the door, and he decided not to enter through the door. Beside it, there was a window, the glass of which was broken, and he entered and took off his shoes at least for keeping silence. There was boundless silence inside and everything was getting more and more silent. He was walking upright, and there was only dust in front of him, rising above the cellar, illuminated by the rays of the moon. The strange silence was getting closer and closer, with the sound of the sand getting stronger and weaker. He turned around, did not notice anything, and went away again. Reaching the staircase that descended to the basement, he felt a warmth behind him, his back began to warm, and he realized that there was something behind him. Pausing for a moment and taking a deep breath, he turned around and noticed a group of people in the dark consisting of sand, as if absorbed in the sand, instead of their skin was sands, and they were looking at him. Adrian was frightened but not lost himself, because he had not done anything yet and noticed a child in the corner who had also been absorbed in the sand but had not fully absorbed his face and he saw himself in that child. That child looked like him very much, that dried face seemed to be his, and Adrian realized that people would do anything with him there, since he was one of them, not absorbed in time yet. Adrian turned again and went down the stairs to the basement. There, he also noticed a group of similar creatures, who had just gathered at the water and wiped their bodies with water. He noticed that pouring the water on their bodies, that sand was temporarily disappearing and the color of their skin started to be visible, but all these were instant. Adrian approached the water bottles, picked up two of the largest from there, and noticed that everyone was just looking at him. It seemed he was strange, not they. He went back full of bottles and stood before the child again. The child smiled at him and approached with his hand soaking in the water filled with these bottles and touched

Adrian with clean skin, which was instantly absorbed in the sand. Adrian came out of the hut and heard the sound of that child behind him.

"Come back."

It was a bright morning and Vam was standing at one of the balconies of the University and was looking at Dwinerd, which was immersed in a great chaos, everywhere was only messy and alarm. What about before you would only hear bird sounds, and you would have time to think with the expectation of making new discoveries.

"Morning has brought you here too early." said Willmah.

"Yes, I tried to come a little early and gather my thoughts before the day will be opened."

"Which kind of connection do have with this town, Vam?" said Willmah, leaning to the balcony and looking at the city.

"What do you mean?"

"Well, what is this town for you, just a piece of land?"

"My whole life is tied to this city." For a moment Vam fell in his thoughts trying to remember the best episodes of his life.

"I was born here, studied, worked, created!" breathing deeply, added.

"Fell in love."

"But is it enough for you to control the heart of this city?" asked Willmah harmoniously.

"I don't know Willmah, to be sincere, I have always been eager to govern, but not knowing that managing is more interesting than serving it, it seems to me that a manager cannot give much if he does not have good servants. Now the city is on the verge of collapse, we have no new scholars who will serve our values. Ralph founded this university on time, which was based on the foundation of the city, and now what, the city is surrounded by people who do not even know why they live here and for what. Before people were serving only for one purpose, the city solved problems in the region, and now what we have, it is just a city, which is gradually destroyed."

"I cannot disagree with you that the city has lost its glory, but for that the ruler must have a great power to restore what has lost."

"And from where can I find that power, Willmah?" Turning to Willmah said Vam and continued.

"May be, you can give me a piece of advice. Dargen was so strong that we only saw that there were no problems, that everything could be solved, but upon his departure I realized that it was simply hidden behind a strong man who would not allow himself to be appeared."

"I know such a fact that what Dargen eliminated will come very soon behind you and behind us," said Willmah.

"If I transfer that material, Sarhat will disappear. Do you understand?"

"And if you don't give, then Dwinerd will disappear. Vam, you have to make a choice, either you have to help your city, or meet Sarhat, which is the city of the persecuted and thousands of innocent people will be the result of that massacre. Now you are the leader of Dwinerd, and you must stand by your people and values, not compassionate your enemy, who has raised hand to you and to us." In response, Vam turned to Willmah and left the balcony looking at him for a moment.

Adrian and the girl were riding to the new horizon, to the capital of the Bright Desert Arishta.

"You say they just weren't there, and you could easily take the water," said the girl, who was also on the horse.

"So, at first it seemed to me that they were there, but I was mistaken there was only sand, and nothing except for it." Said Adrian, who was sitting behind the horse, was watching carefully his hands wrinkled by the bright rays of the sun and continued.

"You did not say what your name is and where you are going."

"You also didn't tell me why you are drying." Looking back for a moment and looking at Adrian's hand, the girl replied.

"Yes! I think it can be the beginning of a good conversation and acquaintance, notwithstanding the small event that happened to us."

"My name is Alia, I'm from Sarhat."

"Hmm…, I've heard about Sarhat, but unfortunately not so good things," He glanced at the dusty horizon.

"Yes, everyone traduces about Sarhat, maybe there are bad people there, but all of that is past. New generations have evolved there over the years and they have as everything as Dwinerd," Noticing dust accumulation in the distance continued,

"People who unwittingly were born in Sarhat become persecuted, but it's wrong and we will fight till the end that such kind of thing happens at all." Turning around and looking at Adrian's face.

"We also have the right to live and to create, and we cannot do it because we are accepted as persecuted, and where are you from?"

"My name is Adrian, I'm from Dwinerd. I haven't always been fond of local scholars, so you can accept me as a friend," said Adrian in a half joke.

"Adrian?" Alia was surprised.

"Yes!"

"It's a long name!" replied quickly and distracted the situation, she continued.

"And where are you going?"

"That's my secret, but since we have met unwittingly and you have wanted to save me without knowing, I think I can tell you my secret."

"It is your right, we will go with different ways soon as we reach the nearest town, and I hope we will not meet again."

"Well, my trip is going to the heart of the desert, and I think yours is too," said Adrian, looking at the girl, and in that moment, Alia turned and noticed that Adrian was gazing at her, and their faces meet each other. Suddenly Adrian noticed the outline of the gates in the distance.

"You see there in the distance?"

"Where?"

"There are gates in the distance!"

"It's not possible to notice the gates so soon..." Not to completing her speech, there was a loud cry, which muffled the whole area.

"What was this?" cried Alia.

"I don't know!" Adrian said.

Around them began a very strong storm, and the road faded into a storm. A few steps away nothing was visible, they just stood waiting for it to be over, but the roar, storm grew stronger, and they mingled. The horse quickly fled from them and they fell to the ground. The storm was so strong that they were absorbed and they were leaving each other.

"Alia!" screamed Adrian and noticed that the girl was almost losing her consciousness. Approaching her somehow, he held her hand and with his only wet piece, which was helping him from drying, covered the girl's face and the girl recovered.

"Look at me!" Alia glanced at Adrian, and noticed huge gates that were opening and the sheer amount of sand coming out of it.

"The gates open!"

"Which gates?" asked Adrian with surprise.

"Behind you," they noticed those gates turning around together.

"We have to go to some solid place to wait for this stream to come to an end, so follow me!"

They ran from the huge gates to the left, where the storm had not yet fully absorbed, and after a long run they reached a rock that was not so difficult to overcome. Adrian gave Alia room to climb up, and he climbed up behind her. Overcoming the rock, they noticed a city merged into the sand, and those gates were located immediately above the gorge, from which a tremendous amount of sand was coming out, as if they had missed it.

"But why are they doing this?" said Alia.

"I don't know. The important thing is we are alive and reached the city!" Confused and amazed at the city, which was seen far from, was so large that the horizon merged with the city. Alia also joined in watching the scene, they had just frozen for a moment.

———— •••• ————

The thunder of the lightning became stronger and stronger, and mount Sarhat, which had endured many trials, was now on the verge of collapse, where Vam and Valmar had met.

"Leave! Valmar, you will be facing death or persecution here," said Vam.

"I met Dargen here last time and he was asking me to tell him something he was not aware of, and now you are asking me to leave to avoid being a victim of persecution."

"Don't you understand that they have that stuff that won't save you from even hiding behind this mountain?"

"They have it or you have given it to them." Looking at Vam's eyes, Valmar said and continued,

"You know what is the difference between me and you?
That I know what I am living for and what I expect from this life, though for some people it sounds bad and strange, but I know for what I am fighting for and behind this mountain I am not just all the people who have been ignored in Dwinerd. You want me to leave them and run at my brother's request," pausing for a moment he gave exact answer.

"I know why I will be persecuted or die."

"I know one thing that they won't yield to anyone who does not meet them," replied Vam, and during that time the lightning struck a couple of blows to the mountain, and they turned away.

"Brother, I've always gone against the people who were against me and this time there is no difference. Let them come, if I have to lose, so it must be."

"I will complete my way and start a new one again with my beliefs, and you will never know what is right or what is wrong" Valmar said, not letting Vam continue his speech.

"Good luck, my brother! Our paths were over."

Saying his last word, Valmar left the mountain rising upward, and Vam, drenched in the rain, just watched how Valmar was leaving, and there was nothing he could do to save himself, as everything had already been done and he had made his decision; for which he regretted, but there was no alternative, otherwise, he was expected the same fortune that would soon follow Valmar. He chose the path of salvation, and Sarhat was overthrown, Ralph's torch was returned to the University, Valmar was sent to the far north for persecution.

CHAPTER IX
Fracture

••••

Ralph's University

Karma and Vam were walking along the sides of mount Sarhat, from which had left almost nothing. Before the mountain was one of the most beautiful sights in the region from where the whole city was seen and the mountain just captivated by its charm, and for years it served as a refuge for the locals and then simply destroyed them.

"When we were children, we were often coming to this place and hiding from everyone, dreaming about becoming a scientist in the future, and now our dreams have come true, but the consequences are not so good," he continued, lifting the stone from the ground.

"I have something to tell you, Karma."

"And what?" asked Karma while walking with him.

Putting the small stones on the ground, Vam looked at the crumbled mountain for a moment and continued.

"Adrian is Ralph's heir."

"How!?"

As he got closer to Vam, Karma said and gazing at Vam continued,

"From where did you get such information?"

Vam continued to walk down the mountain very quietly,

"I called him to my place and handed him a liquid-bottle. During that time, I did not know how, but he was able to pick up one of Ralph's figures.

"What figures are you talking about?" Karma asked, walking alongside with Vam.

"You just won't get those figures, those are wooden figures in the secret room," replied

Vam. Karma was confused trying to understand the content of the conversation and continued,

"And why did you call him to you?" Karma asked pausing their steps and touching on Vam's shoulder to move his face toward him.

"I have taken blood from him and we wanted to seize the power of light together with Valmar by Adrian and to activate the torch."

"Vam, what are you talking about? What you're saying is just awful!" He continued to breathe for a moment.

"In fact, Willmah was right that you used him, and I believed you!"

"It is awful, but you are true, I had better get lost in prison than to live so enclosed in me for my brother's destruction." Looking at the mountain, he continued,

"Everyone should know about it."

Karma was just confused and looking at the ground, her thoughts were elsewhere, raising her head and asked

“And what about Dargen, have you poisoned Dargen!?

"No!"

"I don't even believe you, Vam!" said Karma approaching Vam.

"I hope you'll find you!"

"Karma" Trying to express himself, Karma replied.

"Your words have no meaning for me, I trusted you my heart, but all your deeds were futile!" looking at Vam's eyes for a moment she added.

"Dwinerd has had not ever such a leader!" Karma said and hurried to leave.

——— •••• ———

The city was surrounded with boundless beauty, the locals preserved the rest of the things of the city. They had set up special devices to allow them to filter the air and the environment. They were gathering everything in one place and from time to time releasing large reserves of sand into the desert, so that it did not absorb the city. Alia and Adrian went one of the nearby guesthouses to find a refuge in order to have an opportunity of overnight.

"Hi! Arishta happy to meet you, how can we help you?" asked the worker of the guesthouse.

"We have come a long way and we would like to have the opportunity to spend the night at you," Adrian said.

"Of course, both of you!?" asked the employee.

"Thank you very much, sir, yes, both of us."

The employee noded the assistant and the assistant accompanied them to the room. The room was very small, there was a window at the height of which you had to stand on a chair to see something.

"Anyway we could spend the night outside, the difference wouldn't be much," Adrian made a joke.

"We should not complain, we should be pleased that we have what we have, in the morning we will go with our paths."

They both looked at each other and started to adjust. Adrian removed the figure and placed it on a small table next to the bed. Alia noticed the figure at that moment and looked very carefully, then noticed Adrian's gaze and went back to her work.

"I think we are going to have a very interesting evening," Adrian said, looking at the map carefully, but did not understand it, because the arrows in it were just rotating irregularly, showing no direction, and Alia was just sorting her things and looking at Adrian.

"What's that?" Alia asked.

"A map!" Looking at his map for a moment, Adrian continued.

"But I guess it doesn't work, it's just been a while since the arrows just rotate and don't show anything." And putting it back, he continued.

"Probably they are not working!"

"And from where did you find it?" Alia continued indifferently.

"My friend has transferred me to find the right path, but it looks like just a toy, which gives hope that you're on the right way," Adrian made a joke and noticed the falling sand from the ceiling, which was poured onto the bed.

"What was that?" Adrian surprised and continued.

"And we must overnight here?"

"You're complaining again!" Alia looked out of the window and noticed that as she spoke in a loud voice the sand was pouring there.

"You said there was no difference, if we overnight outside, so, there are all the comforts here!" Alia laughed and continued again.

"I am going out and bring water for us, I think it won't bother us." And Adrian, trying to lie down, noticed the wrinkles growing on him, he was just terrified and looked how Alia was coming out, lay down on the bed.

At the Ralph's University session, only the Experts were present, and the room lit by torches seemed to be dark again, Vam said sitting around a table.

"Dear Council!" Vam, studying all those gathered, was trying to express his thoughts as carefully as possible.

"Today I have invited you all here for something," Withdrawing voice, again continued.

"Valmar was not the only culprit in this situation." All the Experts were just all ears to Vam with interest, it was only Karma, who tried to hide her tears behind her eyes.

"I also helped him in all his evil deeds."

"How!?" Randolph asked in surprise.

"And that is not news for me!" said Willmah."
That you were a traitor, I had felt it for a long time, just nobody believed me or heard me.

"Vam, but how could you do that?" Disappointed, Randolph again said, and Willmah just kept going.

"You persecuted your brother, and your conscience didn't forgive you, of course." In addition, Willmah looked at Vam's depressed and broken face, who had simply forgotten his noble posture.

"And how will your conscience forgive you when Mr. Dargen dies, have you forgotten about it?"

"I'm not guilty poisoning him!" Vam replied shortly.

"Of course, what you need, you are guilty, what exists, you do not accept!" Willmah replied to Vam.

"You must be next to your brother, but unlike you, he has not betrayed and has not wanted to kill his own leader." When Vam saw in the corner how Karma was restraining not to cry, he simply lost the ability to speak and noticed how she was coming out of the room and hurried behind her, but as soon as the door was opened there were University guards who did not let him go out of the room based on Willmah's command. Vam was just following the outline of Karma in the long sunny corridor, and Willmah's voice was heard again.

"Please arrest Mr. Vam!" Coming out of the room and not letting him look at Karma, continued again.

"Before the council convenes the session and understands what the punishment is for the traitor." Vam did not try to traverse and voluntarily surrendered to the guards.

———— •••• ————

In the distance, white light was visible, and Adrian seemed to be flying toward the light, and his hands and body were not visible. It was air or sand or something that could creep in. He did not understand where he was, but his consciousness prompted him that this was not just a dream, but something else that he needed to know and that he was hearing from deep place.

"Come back."

Adrian wakes up and jumps up, then looks around, at the corner of the room, he notices the burning light of a small candle, afterwards turns to the small table and seeing his figure, he has a rest. At that moment, Alia enters with a container full of water in her hand.

"Actually, you can't relax," Adrian said. Alia, putting a water container on the table, replies.

"I'll relax when it's all over and I'll go home."

The sun had already set and they were going to overnight, the beds were two and very small almost side-by-side. Alia also turning off the candle went to bed. The sand was falling from the ceiling of the room because of every loud noise and did not allow Adrian to sleep.

"Hmm…, I thought we would have had a better evening than withstanding this sand rain."

"Well, I think the complaint is the brightest part of your life!" Alia laughed.

"The complaint has always been the start of something that is a positive outcome."

"And what problems have you solved with your complaint?" Alia asked.

"For example, if I were satisfied that we would live without water in the center of the desert and get used to that thought, I might not go to that hut now and we wouldn't be here." Alia just turned to Adrian and didn't say anything, Ad noticed Alia's face and continued.

"Why is such a pretty and charming girl looking for something in these deserts alone for her city?"

"I'm not the first; many have tried to come here, but in vain."

"So, you possess such a knowledge that very few know."

"Something like that!"

"And what are you looking for there, what will this Oasis give you?" Alia thought for a moment and answered.

"I will only tell Queen Arishtha, who will reward me for what I go there, and why are you going there and what are you looking for?"

"I have lost myself. Someone has used me for his own ideas, and my only salvation is to get there and know the answers, otherwise."

"Otherwise what?"

"Otherwise, I might get dust and fall from the ceiling on the people," Adrian laughed.

"I think humor will save you."

"I thought so too." Looking at each other for a moment, Adrian continued.

"Alia, we're heading to the heart of the desert together, let's go there together, I think it will be safer," Alia, listening to Ivy, thought for a moment and answered.

"I think we need to sleep, we've come a long way." Alia said, pausing for a moment and looking straight at the ceiling, then closed her eyes.

Gerberd

In the basement of Ralph's University's central tower, where you could only land with a rope-mounted accessory and climb up the same way. There was a prison cell when it was raining that prison cell was filling with water and only the worst of the weather was visible, and you could only see the rays of the sun in the distance behind the little bars, from where there was hardly any light to penetrate. The prison cell was so cruel that it was specially called Gerberd. The weather was gloomy again outside and it was going to rain. Chained Vam was taken to the central tower. Unlike other towers, reaching that tower you could see swampy stones, which had been absorbed into the wall and become a common particle. When the lightning was illuminating that area, nearby towers were illuminating because of that noise, but not Gerberd, it was so absorbed in impurity and misery that only fire could illuminate it.

————— •••• —————

"Gerberd!" Karma said to Willmah in amazement and continued,

"He dedicated his whole life to the University so that he was thrown to Gerberd."

"The place of all the traitors is in Gerberd!" said Willmah very quietly.

"Yes, he is guilty, but the court has to decide what punishment awaits him and our decision is also very important."

"You're in love." Willmah getting closer said to Karma.

"Maybe," he hung his head down and continued for a moment.

"I was in love, but now it doesn't matter."

"Vam has deserved it all by his own will. He must bear his share of guilt."

"Yes, but after the trial, he could have been placed in an ordinary prison cell, the verdict would have been clear. Then he voluntarily confessed his guilt, he did not deserve such treatment!"

"Well, I can't call back the guards anymore, he's been taken there."

"I'll call them back myself!"

"Karma, by taking such a step you take all the responsibility on yourself, if he escapes, you will be accepted guilty too!" Looking at Willmah and getting angry Karma went out of the room without saying anything.

"Hurry! it's raining hard." Willmah said screaming from behind.

Karma quickly descended the stairs and reached the door, opening it, the wind and rain immediately absorbed her body, and she caught hold of the stair rail for a moment so that her body would not turn. The rain was so heavy that all the drainage cylinders were full and the water was just flooding. Karma, gathering herself for a moment and looking at the sky, waiting for the next thunder of lightning, moved quickly to the tower of central university. Reaching there she was able to open the door, and as she entered, there were loud voices and the sound was alarming as if someone was tormented. Karma taking the nearby torch and lightning it, moved quickly to the corridor of prison cell and noticed anyone, none of the guards was there. Without decelerating her steps she finally reached the abyss where Vam was, but he did not notice Vam, but only the accumulation of water that had filled in that abyss and saw only Vam's garment, which had raised up.

"Vam!" Karma said, immediately released the ropes, and the cart weakened, and she stopped. Wheeling a wooden device hardly, the cart went down into the abyss and reached the end of the abyss where the water was absorbed, she stopped coming down, took the cloth, put it on the cart, and then, looking down at the water, he noticed chained and unconscious Vam. Karma taking out his cloth jumped into the water. The depth of the water was not so much, simply because of chained Vam he could not climb. Karma managed to approach Vam and released the chains somehow, but the air was not enough for her and she went up to breathe the air. Rapidly recharging, she dived again and reached Vam, lifted him on the surface of the water and somehow threw him on the cart. She remained under the water and Vam leaned at the cart. Meanwhile, Karma was caressing Vam's face and was trying to recover his consciousness.

"Vam!" she was simply shouting caressed his face.

"Vam, please, wake up!" said Karma, again caressing and giving artificial respiration. Doing the same thing several times there was no difference; Vam's body was immobile and was not subject to Karma's tortures. Losing her power for a moment Karma just hugged Vam and said,

"Please, breathe!" And gave him respiration again, but this time she gave deeper breath, and all of a sudden Vam's consciousness came back and Karma hugging him very strong just cried. Her tears were filling into the abyss under the rain, which swallowed everything that fell into it.

In the morning, Adrian opened his eyes quickly and did not notice Alia, then turned to the small table and did not notice his figure and the priest's utensils. Getting up and not seeing

Alia's packages, he realized that Alia had left without him. Gathering the rest of the things Adrian hastily tried to find the map, which Dan had given him and noticed that the arrows in the map were again rotating irregularly. Ad was just surprised for a moment, put it back and came out of the room quickly. As he opened the door, he noticed that everything that had been there the day before the bright room, the corridor, and the guesthouse was in a state of decay. There was sand everywhere, behind which the parts from interior were outlined with very difficulty as if you had come another world. Adrian was puzzled for a moment and realized that he had already seen all these, and going ahead the ground started to crumble from under his feet. Ad began to run, reaching the staircase, tried to jump, approached the edge he was able to catch, and his feet were completely immersed in the sand. The sand began to pull back him, and he was gradually absorbed in that sand. Looking for a moment, he noticed the table in front of him and stretched out at the foot of that table, but the wooden leg was very thorny, and his hands began to tremble. The strength of his hands didn't satisfy him and gradually he dived into the sand. He took off his jacket and tied it to the foot of that table, began to pull himself out of the sand with the help of a strong hand and a piece of cloth. He stubbornly managed to get out of that sand. He quickly emerged to the door and noticed that the door was already absorbed by these strange sand particles and it was useless to open it in the usual way. He took a few steps back and realized that going back was also useless. For a moment, he took a deep breath, ran straight to the door, and broke the sand into the door. He came out from the other side and fell out, where there was nothing but red sky and sand, where there were small storms in places and all looked like hell. There was a very loud, occasional girl screaming, which was absorbing a sense of fear in her body. Adrian was somehow looking for a sketch of the road in a storm so that he could at least be guided somewhere, and suddenly he saw one of the priest's items thrown to the ground in the distance. Against the backdrop of those sands, it was just a contrast it was a glass jar of water, and Adrian somehow managed to reach the container with his hands and saw it finished, and the wrinkles on his body were spreading rapidly sooner or later he would become a part of it too. Looking at that container for a long time, he cried.

"Alia..." he took a few steps forward and screamed again,

"Alia!" But his voice only softened the stock of all the energy that had accumulated in him and nothing else was happening. Going ahead a little, he noticed strong light reflections in the distance and unwittingly began to go there and to hear a familiar voice.

"Come back."

He began to approach the light as he heard it, and his voice became clearer. He realized that the sound was coming from the depth of that light and it was not a dream. Suddenly a great abyss began to appear beneath his feet, and he hastened his steps to the light. The closer he got to that light, the more the abyss was growing behind him. If he had stopped, he would have fallen, so he would have run so strong that if there was something in front of him, he would have just collapsed rather than stopped. Upon reaching that light, he noticed a square building of symmetrical white stone, around which the sand seemed to be the blood of that building. In the middle of the bright white building, there was a single piece of stone, and it was not hard to see that the stone was not in its place. As he approached the piece of stone, he noticed the little boy, whom, he had seen in the hut, and who had told him to come back. He recognized the child at once, and h was simply pointing at Adrian that he would slash the stone and throw it into the place. Adrian approached the stone very quietly, looked at the child, and then shook the stone by hand. The stone just leveled the wall. When Adrian turned around, he did not notice the child, and then he turned around and saw that there was a corridor in front of him. He had nothing left but to go straight there; he knew that all this might be just a dream, but his consciousness told him another thing. Going straight for a long time, he finally noticed a small rock from which water was flowing. There he stopped and looked down and saw a round stone table, which reminded a rock, below which was very clean water, which was filled from that rock, and there were various items on the stone table. Not far from the table, he noticed Alia, in front of whom Ralph's figures were also lying on the ground, and the piece given to him by the priest was in Alia's hands.

"Alia!" Ad said softly and tried to get down, but when he approached the edge of the rock, a protective layer of water came in front of him, which he encountered and was unable to move. After a few attempts, Ad ran out and knelt down, putting her hands on his head. For a moment he tried to gather his thoughts and understand what was going on, lowering her hands to his face, he noticed a bright light in front of him that did not hurt his eyes at all, and from there a woman's voice was heard. "Finally, we met!"

CHAPTER X
Arishta

••••

Desert Storm

Alia was lying on the ground and without losing her consciousness completely, realized that the sound of a storm was coming from the abyss that would soon swallow her. She was trying to get up, while Adrian was following Alia from above.

"This is a dream." said Adrian, looking at Alia, who was resisting a sandstorm down from a thin layer of water.

"Almost!" said the woman's voice from the light.

"I don't understand anything."

"You are on the opposite side of your imagined world."

"What do you mean?"

"That is to say, you are in my world, Adrian, and I have waited for this meeting for a long time."

"I see those things, which don't exist."

"You see those things, which aren't there."

"And how can I get out of here?"

"You have come so long way to appear here. All the experts give their lives so that they can appear here, and you wish to leave. I will tell you all the wonders of Arishta, if you stay here and serve the sand kingdom."

"Everything is wonderful here," but looking at Alia for a moment, who did not know what to do, he continued,

"My place is there!"

"Love, of course, is a very strong feeling, and it breaks the broken people, or vice versa, gives strength to the broken people. You are the only Wise Expert, who has come here, so I will give you what you have come for."

"Life!" Ad said, thinking and looking at Alia for a moment.

"Life, but what is life when there is eternal life?"

"You said that I am one of the worthy people who has managed to get here, but why just me?"

"There are many roots in your blood, and it comes from far away. You don't know who you are."

"And who am I?"

"You are the heir of Ralph, the most realistic Expert who will have ever given Darwar to Dwinerd."

"But I don't feel myself like that."

"It doesn't matter what you feel, it the most important thing is what's inside you."
Adrian, looking around for a moment, noticed sand particles in the air that were rotating around him. Then he looked over to Alia's side, around which there was also a hurricane of sand, and he said.

"I feel you..."

"They are part of you Adrian, nature is in you and you feel them!" The hurricane seemed to be subjected to Ad and an adventurous thought came to his mind, doing that he was not sure that everything would go well, but he felt it was the right way and said in a harmonious voice.

"Arishta, I want to go back!"

"That's your decision, and I'll reward it to you, but only one person can get out of here." Said the voice coming from the light. Adrian approaching the protective layer of water and looking to Alia's side, noticed a hurricane that would soon engulf Alia, as it had swallowed all those who had come for their ideas, but it had been in vain. Ad turned opposite to light and opening his hands as the rays of the stars, he said.

"I don't think so!" he closed his eyes and just said in his mind.

"I feel you!"

The hurricane, which swallowed up everything around it, seemed to have become one body with Adrian. Ad felt his body tearing from the ground and heading to the direction, where the sand particles would lead him, and finally merging with the storm, Adrian said.

"Alia, put the figure in the center of the table!"

It was a very strong storm around Alia, but she heard Adrian's voice and somehow found strength in her took the figure, approached the center of the table, just focused on the figure and exploded, but it did not come out of the figure, just remained there as a light. Alia fell down again, losing her last strength, and suddenly a voice was heard behind her.

"Alia..." the hands of the solid man turned to Alia and lifted her up. She only saw the image of a faded man in front of her exhausted face, and that image became clearer gradually, she realized that it was Ad and Alia just uttered his name.

"Adrian."

CHAPTER XI
Return

••••

Ralph's University

Dargen's bed was in the middle of the room and a large window was opened on the right side, where the sun was coming in and the room was softly lit. Although the room was very light and warm, Dargen's body was absorbed by the blue shade, which did not allow it to open and illuminate with the colors of the room. Suddenly the door was opened and Dan entered, who approached Dargen and looked at his swampy body that was still enduring the evil.

"It's a pity that I should do it," he said, getting closer his hand to Dargen's face and gently pressing his mouth, from where the oxygen was coming, which was the sole impetus for the preservation of life. Meanwhile, the door was opened again and Karma came in. Dan raised his hand quickly and stroked Dargen's face.

"Dan, what are you doing here?" She surprised and came across to Dargen, trying to open the window to get in.

"Mrs. Karma." Dan said without hesitation, and continued.

"Dargen, my teachers, and me just couldn't be next to him!" Looking at Dargen and slowly pulling his hand, Dan concluded.

"Yes, that is why come down and bring some water to refresh Mr. Dargen's skin." Karma said, approaching Dargen and looked attentively at Dan.

"Of course!" Dan said, leaving the room, and Karma looking at Danny strangely, noticed how he was coming out, then opened the window and stroked Dargen's head gently.

Alia and Adrian were returning north from the Bright Desert, Sarhat. The sky was cloudy, but the rain was not rushing to fill the region with its drops, but just a bluish hue everywhere, blending with the damp green, creating a gloomy atmosphere.

"I'll show you the good parts of Sarhat," Alia said on the horse, and as if not noticing the effect of the gloomy weather, her soul was so warm on the event of returning to her native land.

"You will see how people live and everything is not as good as you were told in the Dwinerd."

Unlike Alia Adrian was exploring around him and became gloomy because of the gray weather, but he smiled, not allowing the gloom to absorb him. Reaching mount Sarhat, they noticed the ruined mountain as if it were halfway between the mountains. Alia got off the horse, run to the mountainside quickly, and stopped for a moment, slowly landing on the ground, picked up the muted flower that was only growing on these places, looked up at the mountain and began to cry. Approaching Alia and hugging her, Adrian said.

"Nothing will happen to us in Sarhat, come with me to Dwinerd."

"No!" Alia continued, gathering her thoughts and standing for a moment.

"I was born here and we have to go there."

Alia climbed to the mountain quickly, and Adrian screamed behind her.

"The mountain is ruined, if we enter there we can be destroyed by pieces of stone!" Ad noticed that Alia was not subject to him, hurried to follow her.

"No! I must go there." Alia said very slowly going ahead.

"So, I'll come with you!" Adrian said, joining Alia, and the latter looked at Adrian and hugged her tightly. They came in the ruined mountain, where large pieces of stones were hung from the air that could be shaken by the sound of the wind, but they did not worry about anything, they wouldn't hurt anybody. Walking a bit into the dark cave, Alia told Ad.

"This was our home!" Alia went on touching the stone pieces.

"There are so many memories here that have been leveled to the ground." Adrian was simply following Alia and exploring the area to avoid danger.

"Unfortunately, I can't show you the beauty that was here." Alia continued to tell him with her tearful eyes.

"I see it walking with you. Everything is beautiful for me, when I am with you," Ad replied.

Walking a long way and reaching the end of the stone tunnel, they noticed military forces in the distance, coming toward them on horseback, they hid behind piles of nearby stones, and those military forces passed by them. Adrian noticed the sign on them that he had seen also in Dwinerd.

"I think this is a royal army." Adrian said behind the hidden stones.

"But they couldn't enter here!" Alia said angrily and running out of stones, ran to the military forces.

"Come back!" Ad screamed behind Alia.

"You have destroyed what was created by nature!" Alia said breathlessly, throwing stones at the horse. A group of royal soldiers stood up and noticed them, they moved back quickly, and Adrian came out, held Alia's hand, and said.

"Run after me!"

They began to flee out of the cave, and as soon as they reached the exit, they reached Sarhat, but they noticed huts coming out of the smoke and burning houses and nobody was there. Alia ran to the nearby hut, it was her father's home, not far from the entrance to the mountain. When she arrived, she noticed that the house was ruined and started crying,

"Mother... Father!" But hearing no voice, Alia entered the house and took her father's sword, came out quickly, but Adrian did not let her go.

"No! Alia..." Ad was trying to calm down Alia,

"You will change nothing. They are much more and more armed we will not be able to resist."

"At least I'll do something," Alia replied, confronting to Ad.

"No, calm down!" Adrian said, trying to hug and soothing Alia, but in vain. The anguish that had accumulated in her was not still leaving Alia's body. The armed group approached, surrounded them and took as hostage. They were taken to a nearby area where the hostages were held and tied to a cylindrical wooden pillar of a nearby tent room.

——— •••• ———

Alia had just closed her eyes for a moment, she was trying to have a rest, to realize everything and was hearing Adrian's conversation with the soldiers. Afterwards everything kept silence.

"You know, they haven't left anything." Tied to the pillar Alia continued.

"Meanwhile, I was looking for such kind of thing in the desert, which would save us, but I was to be here, and the result is, that I couldn't even help them." Trying to answer Alia, all of a sudden Ad saw in the distance that the shred of the tent was being opened and a man was coming in. His face became visible from the bosom of light and Adrian recognized that man.

"Dan!?" Adrian asked, moving his body a little, which was tied to the pillar.

"Hey... Adrian!" Approaching quickly, Dan replied and went on,

"You have been saved!"

"So, as you see, I am hostage again." Ad replied with half-smile.

"We may always meet like that."

"Release him," Dan ordered.

"As well as Alia!" Ad went on shortly.

"Sorry, but I am not able to release her, she is one of Valmar's experts, and we must send all the experts of Sarhat to persecution."

"In that case, I'll be also persecuted!" Not allowing the military to touch him, Ad continued.

"And you won't know where the light is."

"Ad, don't you understand that lots of things have changed here."

"Dan, you don't understand either." Ad said, looking straight into his eyes.

"Lots of things have changed too!" Thinking for a moment he went on.

"You release me and Alia and I will give the light, cause she has helped me find it and bring me here, and you want to send that person to persecution who has promoted to everything."

"You're so tricky! Adrian." Dan went on looking at Alia,

"Well, I'll release you, but first of all you must give me the light." Turning to Adrian again Dan said.

"The light is in my pocket, take it." Ad replied shortly, and Alia was just following Danny's steps, trusting Adrian. Dan getting closer to Adrian, checked his pockets and noticed a figure wrapped in the priest's cloth.

"Hmm…, actually you are really Ralph's inherit!" Holding the cloth in his hand that lowering and taking the figure from inside Dan continued.

"Everything comes from your gene." He said, looking at the figure for a long time and took it with him.

"Release them, but you can't stay any longer here. Now, this area is under the king's control and you have to return Dwinerd and see Willmah."

"We must see Willmah?" Ad said trying to break the ties.

"Yes, he manages the University now. I think he would like to talk to you, who found the light and returned from all the bright desert." Dan following for a moment how he was being released, he left the tent.

———— •••• ————

The sky was cloudy again and the wind was moving with the opposite direction in Dwinerd. There was an unusual coldness in the city as if everything was good, however everything was going bad. The city guards had begun to be extremely cruel to the local people and punished them for every small mistake. The bright city had been transformed into a cold and cruel environment. Alia and Adrian were at the threshold of Ralph's University, they were going to enter to meet Willmah.

"How many events are connected with the name Adrian" Willmah said sitting in a long chair, which was in the middle of the hall.

“Yes, sir!" Looking at Alia and then going ahead to Willmah, Ad continued.

"Many events have been in my life, and I am glad that it has happened for the benefit of the University and the city."

"And what about the girl, who was with you?" Looking at Alia for a moment Willmah said.

"Will you introduce her?"

"I'm Alia." Alia said, and came across to Adrian.

"I am from Sarhat and I have served that city, which exists no longer now."

"Yes!" Willmah raised his voice a little, stood up and continued.

"Sarhat hasn't existed, it has been a city of persecutors, and now the persecutors are in their proper place." Willmah came across to them with Ralph's torch in his hand. Alia and Adrian unwittingly looked down as a sign of respect.

"And what about Mr. Vam?" Adrian asked, raising his head and looking at Willmah.

"When I was escaping, he was managing the University."

"Yes! He confessed that he had been behind all evils, and he had just used you to reach and possess the light, and his fortune would soon be obvious." Getting closer to them Willmah continued quietly.

"Why are we talking about bad things, everything is in the past, I just wanted to see you and reward your work," Putting his hand on Adrian's shoulder and taking out the special friendship sign of the University Willmah gave it Adrian.

"Sir! I serve my people and my city. This was just like living for me," Ad continued becoming sober.

"And the only reward is that the city is alive and people are healthy, I don't want any reward."

"You are real Dwinerd man, I think the given label of the quack wasn't appropriate for you!" lowering his hand from Adrian's shoulder Willmah said.

"Sir, the evil people were doing that, to discredit my name!"

"What would you like the University to do for you?"

"Respected Willmah, I would like to go back home and continue my activity with my beloved," Ad said, looking at Alia, and Willmah looked at Alia too and answered.

"You are a smart guy! I wish you a welcome. The doors of the University are always open to you," nodding to his companions to guide them.

"Sir, I have a request," Keeping silence for a moment and noticing Willmah's positive gesture, Ad continued.

"I would like to see Mr. Vam before leaving, as I have many questions to ask him, and then I can return to the course of my quiet life to continue serving my people."

"Of course!" Willmah said, nestling on his chair.

"The guards will guide you!" Hearing Willmah's answer Alia and Adrian left the room.

———— •••• ————

Coming out of the courtroom, Alia and Ad were guided to the ward of university by the guards and they saw Karma on their way, who was just coming out of Dargen's restroom. Ad noticed depressed Mr. Dargen in the distance, who was lying and his body was decomposed. It seemed very strange and familiar to Adrian. Finally overcoming the string of stairs, they approached to Vam, and Adrian glanced at Alia and made hint that he would go there alone. Entering the ward besides light rays of the sky and the depressed man in the dark corner, there was nothing else in the ward.

"Hi, my friend!" Vam said and continued standing up from the corner.

"Look, where the path of your life brought you," Vam continued, looking at himself.

"I think it isn't completed yet." Ad replied without hesitation.

"Oh, no, it isn't completed, of course." Shying to look at Adrian, Vam turned to little bars from where the light was hardly coming into the ward.

"You will still have a lot to do, and I won't have, unfortunately.

"Why exactly me?" approaching Vam, Ad said.

"How did you know?"

"I don't know, my friend, we were just following the progress of the city and noticed you," Vam said, looking at the blue cloudy sky.

"But you've served the council so many years, why did behave like that?"

"I've made a lot of mistakes in my life," Falling into his thoughts for a moment Vam continued.

"It is my true decision of my life that I did." Saying that Vam went to the corner, where benches of outworn wood were for one person, and he sat there.

"But you will be beheaded!"

"Let me go, I'm ready!" Vam said quietly.

"You're stupid, my friend!' Ad said, turning to the bars.

"That you were thinking of poisoning Mr. Dargen and being in his place."

"I think they tried to behave me as a fool," looking straight Vam said.

"Maybe I was too cruel, but not a fool."

"You mean you haven't poisoned him," Adrian turned to Vam again.

"Whom it will help, my friend, the result is what we have."

"You are accused of treason and intoxication, without accusation of intoxication you will be sent to persecution but you won't beheaded!"

"And why a man so worried for me whom I have betrayed myself and sent to death?"

"If you weren't," Ad continued thinking for a moment.

"I would not meet the meaning of my life and had not recognized myself, and you showed me automatically the right direction."

"Yes, but it's all over. Willmah was much more forehanded and won me in this war," Vam said.

"Have a nice trip! good luck, my friend."

"How has Mr. Dargen been poisoned?" Adrian asked sharply. Vam left the dark side of the ward without saying a word, and Adrian came out of the ward, realizing that Vam was unable to speak.

——— •••• ———

Returning home Adrian noticed that everything was in mess in his laboratory, being exhausted, he didn't want to move anything and sat down at his desk. He was just looking at the cupboard in front of him for a moment, which contained his exposed liquids and the image of Dargen was in his mind, whom it was hard not to notice his body had been so persecuted that it was differentiated from other things in the distance. Adrian understood that something was wrong, but he could not understand what it was. Later Alia came into his workplace and behind her was her dog Wil, which was just playing with Alia with great pleasure.

"You could say that you have such a beautiful dog and I would fall in love with you just for that." Alia said to Adrian thoughtfully approaching him.

"I'm not looking for easy ways!" Ad laughed.

"Yes, you love to make things complicated." Alia continued, and they looked at each other, and during that time the dog began to scent something in the ragged things and began to bark, then scented again, and noticing all that Ad said.

"What's up Wil, why are you barking?" the dog was going on to dig a long section where things were scattered, approaching it Ad said again.

"What have you found there?" Coming closer to the dog, Ad leaned and lifted the books from the ground, and he saw a figure of a wooden horse scattered in the depth of books.

"Hmm…," Adrian said holding in his hand, studying the figure.

"It seems to me that I've already seen this figure somewhere."

"What's that?" Alia surprised joining Ad too.

"A wooden figure!" Looking attentively at it Ad continued.

"Which was in Danny's hand, when we were going to north, Ad uttered the last word too loudly, as if he understood something and came across to his table quickly, and the dog was behind him.

"Wil, good for you!" Stroking the head of the dog, he put the figure on the table, and the dog was very proud just sitting on the ground, taking his tongue out of his mouth.

"But why is that figure in your house?" Alia surprised.

"I don't know. I don't like this everything. I felt that something was wrong, but it couldn't be so deep." Seated on the chair and his regard in uncertainty, Adrian said.

"I don't know, but there are many questions."

Approaching Ad and taking the figure, Alia began to explore it and said.

"I think there is a very forehanded man behind all this." Alia muttered. Adrian was in his thoughts and suddenly he raised his head listening Alia's words. He turned to her side and looking attentively said to her.

"Forehanded!" Adrian uttered that word as if he had won something and rejoiced for it.

"What?" Alia surprised.

"You said he was a forehanded man!" Ad continued again.

"Yes! and what?" Alia did not quite understand.

"And who is the most forehanded man in this town?" Ad asked.

"Ad, I don't know, what do you mean?"

"Willmah!" Adrian said.

"He's the most forehanded man in this town."

"But he wanted to reward and help you."

"Yes, that's exactly what I mean, Alia," Coming closer to the girl, he approached the table and instructed that they sit down together and continue.

"Let's go to the beginning!" Adrian said.

"They wanted the girl to get sick."

"Which girl?" Alia surprised.

"Her name was Hanna, there was a girl who was sick, but actually she was poisoned, that no one was able to heal her, and everyone thought she was sick," Ad told with bright eyes, and Alia listened very attentively to Adrian.

"Then they already knew who I was and they made me deliberately participate in that treatment. However, they knew that Vam was also interested in me, so they would offer me the liquid I needed and put everything on me, afterwards they would make Vam and Valmar leave."

"And for what?" Not understanding Adrian's words, Alia asked.

"They would have been eliminated without you."

"No, they needed the light!"

"The light! Which you gave to that boy." Alia laughed.

"Now it is at Willmah!"

"Right!" Ad replied very happily.

"So, Adrian, you are the most stupid man in the world."

"Yes, but there is one big problem that I realized during this time," looking at Alia Ad continued.

"Sometimes the strongest side of people can become the weakest and most vulnerable place."
Noticing Alia's thoughtful face, who was trying to understand Adrian, the latter continued again.

"I know how to treat Mr. Dargen."

CHAPTER XII
Refraction

....

Dungeon

It seemed that the sun was not going to appear in the Dwinerd, and that dark and gloomy weather continued to occupy the entire sky of Darwar attempting to show that Darwar and general Dwinerd are under his rule and that the bright weather was not in a hurry to brighten that region. The prison cell of the Ralph's University, which once existed simply as a symbolic phenomenon, currently it was the most talked-about place and was in the center of the actions, it seemed as though its role was more important than the essence of the University itself. And now the prison cell doors were opening again, and Karma was coming down to Vam.

"Why are you leaving just when I need you so much?" said Karma beyond the bars, unwilling to enter.

"What do you mean Karma?" asked Vam sitting in the corner.

"I mean the life that we have created," said Karma harmoniously and disappointed, and continued,

"Which I am going to take alone now."

"You're pregnant!" said Vam getting up from the corner and getting closer to Karma. Karma noticed Vam's face that was not visible in the dark corner, but the light began to illuminate it, when he got closer and the image was worn out, and the old, fresh, confident face that used to express Vam's noble presence was now gone. There was only a persecuted one. And it seemed as if he was an image, which found its place and was in harmony with him.

"What does it matter now?" replied Karma.

"I'm the most unfortunate person in the world, who betrayed his brother, his leader," pulling out his hands out of bars, he lightly touched Karma's hand and continued.

"As well as to his beloved person." Vam said depressed and continued removing his hand again.

"Go Karma! I hate myself."

Karma was watching with tearful eyes how his beloved man got locked up in a dark corner, who was once so noble and self-confident man, but she could not help him and for the last time just fixing Vam's thoughtful eyes to remember it and then, left Vam with great difficulty. Sitting in the corner Vam was thinking only of one thing, when the time would come that he would no longer feel and notice what was happening to him, what's going on inside him, but in all of this there was truth for Vam and no matter how strange it may sound, there was clarity, clarity towards his future, even though it should have been shorter, but cleaner. The fate of life should have been so cruel to him, but he was happy with that fate, because there was no betrayal, no deception, nothing that would destroy him, and destroy during his existence and the death would be his only salvation.

——— •••• ———

Sitting in a dark corner for a long time, Vam suddenly noticed beyond the bars how a strange man, who had thrown an old garment at him so as not to be seen, approached him. He had already imagined in his mind the only guest, which could be the death, who would come after him and show the way, and a voice was heard.

"Mr. Vam!"

"What?" Vam asked amazed, becoming sober for a moment by the word Mister.

"Mr. Vam, that's me Ad," said Adrian, throwing back his headscarf.

"Adrian?" Vam came up to the bars surprised.

"Yes!"

"But how did you get in?"

"I have a good memory, how they got me out of this building," looking around him, continued Ad.

"In the same way I came to you," he concluded smiling.

"Nothing will save me Adrian, you came here for nothing."

"Excuse me, of course, I respect you, but I did not come for you," said Adrian, looking around not to be noticed.

"So why have you come?" Vam asked in surprise.

"I know how to save Mr. Dargen."

"It is impossible to save him, my friend. Everyone has tried to heal him, but to no avail."

"Hmm…," Compressing his lips and looking straight into Vam's eyes, Adrian continued.

"I think I've already heard such expression," said Adrian with a smile.

"But I need the liquid you've given me once."

"I don't have anymore, there either, but wait! Karma." For a moment, recalling Karma the wrinkles on Vam's face were inadvertently stretched.

"Yes." said Ad, waiting for the continuation.

"Karma will help you! she's one of the scholars of this University, go to her and say," After a moment, Vam continued,

"Tell her that I sent you and she will help you," Once again, becoming thoughtful.

"Tell her, for the sake of our overall happiness, she'll understand."

"Thank you very much, Mr. Vam!" smiling and expressing hope to Vam Adrian prepared to leave.

"I thank you!" following how Adrian was leaving, he continued.

"Adrian."

Adrian heads to the security room of the University enters there without worrying and realizes that they did not even notice him.

"Hmm…, " said Ad.

"Who are you and why are you here?" The guards quickly approached him.

"My name is Adrian!" and he continued showing the sign given by Willmah,

"I think Mr. Willmah have presented me very vividly."

Hearing the word Willmah, the guards sobering up and, for a moment, just exchanged looks, Ad continued with a smile.

"That the doors are open in front of me."

"The boy is telling the truth!" Said one of the guards.

"One minute!" said Ad.

"I think we are familiar, and I've come here once." And hiding smile from his face.

"But you did not welcome me so warmly!"

"It is our duty, sir!"

"Well, if you don't want Mr. Willmah to know about it, please accompany me to the Honorable scholar Karma," thinking for a moment Ad continued.

"I have a discovery and would like to introduce it."

A group of guards prepared to accompany Adrian without hesitation and while they were going up the stairs, Adrian was walking behind the guards and he noticed that the guard in the bottom were bringing in a girl and looking very carefully, she noticed that it was Alia.

"Silly girl..." Adrian said in his mind.

They went up the stairs, and one of the guards said.

"The front door, beyond the pillars!" and when the guards turned, Adrian was gone and one of them noticed that the keys to the chains were missing.

•••

They were taking Alia to the University prison with her hands chained and when they reached the front of the bars, have stopped for a moment to open the front door and be able to continue their way. While Alia was leaving, she noticed Adrian sitting next to one of the columns, who was watching closely and smiling lightly. Alia was confused for a moment and looked away, but then, looking at the same spot, she didn't notice anyone. They escorted Alia into one of the prison cells, and then locked the door with bars. In front of Alia was a wet wall against which the sun was shining with its reddish hues.

"Hey!" Alia suddenly heard a familiar voice behind the bars. Alia did not notice anyone looking right and left, and then she heard a door crack and the door opened, Ad came up to him.

"I told you to wait outside!" said Ad, trying to release Alia.

"I don't like to wait as you know," Alia said, looking closely into Ad's eyes.

"What a pity!" Adrian continued, finally releasing the girl.

"Now, if we don't run away from here, you'll definitely wait a long time." They rushed to leave the area and went out to the prison corridor, where two guards were standing behind. They had to reach that intersection to cross the corridor so that they could get out and slowly approaching that intersection, they were able to turn around and no one noticed them. But as soon as they turned one of the guards was standing right in front of them and the guard noticed them and approached them and they fled back. As soon as they got to the intersection, the two guards were waiting for them there, too, and they had to wait and see what would happen. They approached them, twisted their hands, and again, tried to take them to the prison. In the meantime, they saw Karma coming down to the prison and they confronted the scholar for a moment.

"Mrs. Karma!" said one of the guards.

"Who are they, and why are you taking them there?" Looking surprised at Alia and Adrian inquired Karma.

"They came in illegally and tried to run away."

"No, they're cheating!" Ad said, and continued,

"We're here to see you," one of the guards twisted Adrian's hand tighter.

"To see me, and why?" Karma wondered, and Ad looking for a moment into the guards' eyes, then looked down at Karma's chest and slowly raising his head continued.

"The happiness that is with you, no one knows about it but I know. I have a discovery that will interest you." Adrian concluded, and Karma realized that they had something to say and did not want to speak out in the presence of the guards.

"These people are my friends, gentlemen." thinking for a moment said Karma.

"How!?" one of the guards was surprised.

"But they…" Karma replied sharply.

"Yes! and that's no way to meet friends," said Karma roughly, and the guards let them both out without hesitation.

"Excuse me! Mrs. Karma, they just seemed too dangerous, and we considered it appropriate…" not managing to conclude the speech Karma continued again.

"Yes! and now you know that they have come to me," she continued following how Alia and Adrian stood next to her. Exchanging glances for a moment, everyone went their own ways.

The old man was preparing the next Great Meeting candle in the special University room. Waiting long for the end of the fire, he opened the flaming door, from which he pulled out the iron bowl on which the candle was still reddish and had failed to dry. He took it and placed it on the bowl. The candle was so clean that if you looked very closely you could see outlined images behind it. After the final wipe, the old man placed it on a moving cart and headed to the boardroom.

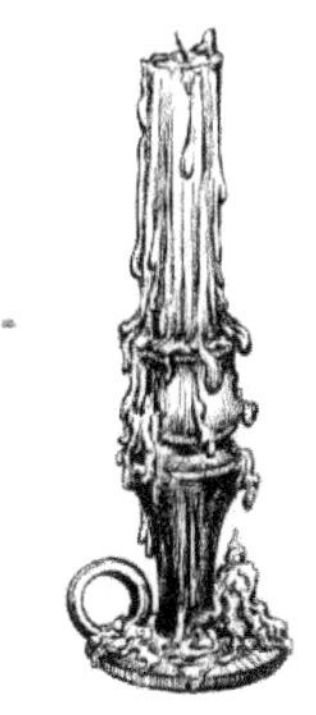

CHAPTER XIII
Great Gathering

••••

Ralph's University

There was no one in the gathering room yet, but everything was already there to organize their Gathering. The torches hanging on the walls illuminated so as not to interfere with the main purpose. And Willmah and his assistant Dan came first. Willmah had waited for the day of heading the gathering too long. He sat firmly near the table holding Ralph's torch in his hand. And Dan was standing very proudly next to him. They were waiting for the arrival of the rest of the Connoisseurs. Next,

Randolph came into the room, staring at Dan and the torch firmly pressed into Willmah's hand.

"Karma is late!" said Willmah.

"Today's Great Gathering is of great importance, and we must raise many issues."

"Karma is always late!" said Randolph, looking at them. The candle had already been placed in the center of the table, and for a moment everyone was looking at it, and it seemed as if that candle looked more dignified than all the people gathered there.

"If Karma doesn't come, we will both run the Gathering," said Willmah.

"Willmah! The law doesn't allow to do that." Randolph replied sharply.

"You know it very well."

"If it goes on in such a manner, I'll change it!" said Willmah, looking at the candle, and after a moment the doors opened, and Karma entered as well, joining quietly the Connoisseurs gathered around the table.

"Excuse me for being late!" Karma said indifferently, sitting on her chair.

"Well, let's get started!" Willmah said, and glancing over at Dan and he showing that he should burn the fire of the torch. Willmah took it and approached to the candle to light.

Very slowly he approached the torch to the side of the candle and the connoisseurs were looking after the process. And as he touched the very thin and white thread that came out of it, he saw that it was not obeying him. And that thread was as white as it was as if nothing had happened with the candle and the candle had not been activated.

"Hmm…," Willmah faltered.

"The old man probably didn't prepare well this time." He finished his talking pulling back the torch.

"It can't be like that!" Karma noticed, and Randolph continued.

"No such case has been registered." Everyone looked at each other in amazement, and Randolph again said.

"So, everything is too bad!"

"I'll try again..." said the opinionated Willmah. And again, nothing succeeded, and he was furious and ordered Dan to activate it.

"An ordinary young man cannot light the candle. He is not high enough to take part in a gathering!" said Karma, standing from her seat up, and continued her speech.

"It is only the Leader's responsibility!" Looking intently into Willmah's eyes, she continued.

"So you're not our leader, if the candle goes against you, then we all have nothing to do in this University." Karma got angry and looked at Randolph, who was attentively listening to her.

"I'll try once again," said Willmah in a more frightened voice.

"That's enough!" Randolph said.

"I resign my position and suggest that we all shall resign and the University temporarily suspend its work until the matter is resolved." And Willmah noticed that the connoisseurs wanted to leave the meeting room and angrily shouted,

"No! Without you or with you, I will manage this University, and no candle will interfere with me," Willmah stood up bumping the torch to the ground and concluded.

"But Randolph is right, if you can't light a candle, then everything is worse than we can imagine. The University doesn't exist as much as we are sitting here," Karma noticed and Randolph headed to the door. But Willmah screamed angrily at them and dropped the torch again.

"No one will come out of this room! While I am here. You will either obey me or you will be persecuted." The whole fire seemed to have accumulated in the eyes of Willmah, which looked so cruel and full of deep disappointment.

"Together! With Valmar." he took out the light Dan had taken from Adrian and lifted it up.

"What is that?" Karma and Randolph asked in surprise, and they didn't rush out.

"This is something with the help of which all of you will obey me," Willmah said very loudly and proudly. He get it closer to the torch of Ralph to activate it and everyone was staring at him and not understanding what was happening, but they realized that the combination of these two things would never lead to anything good. And they didn't imagine what would happen if the light touched the torch. Suddenly a sound was heard.

"Put it back! Willmah." It was a harsh, half-pitched sound that warmed the gathering and the torches hanging on the walls seemed to burn brighter whereas their intensity did not increase.

"Dargen..." Willmah asked in surprise and turned a little frightened.

"Get it back, don't do that!" again that voice, and from the back of the room, at the second secret doorway, Dargen came in front of the table, followed by Adrian.

"But you..." Astonished look at Dargen. And now the fire in his eyes was frozen and looked like an ice that could crumble at any moment.

"How…"

"I tell you to put the light back!" Dargen said in a loud voice, and repeated.

"Willmah!" when Dargen called someone's name it seemed that he entered into him, and the man who heard his name was immediately sobered by Dargen.

"No! I'm not going to put it back, I'll get it done." This time Willmah's response wasn't so convincing.

"Not everything is so clear," said Adrian, coming forward to be more visible. He palpated the water container in his hand, which was given by the priest. There was a flash of bright light.

"You would never have been able to hold that figure in your hands," Dargen said confidently, getting closer to Willmah again, this time more relaxed.

"Coming to power was above all for you. For a moment you have even overestimate your own strength.

"But..." fear had already captured Willmah and was speaking instead of him.

"Nothing, but!" And turning to the other connoisseurs, Dargen continued.

"Since today I am suspending the Great Gatherings until we have five connoisseur members. And in that case, we shall meet after which we shall understand its necessity."

"Yes! Mr. Dargen," said Randolph and Karma simultaneously, and there was a glimmer of hope on their faces that had not been so much on their faces. Karma did not restrain her results.

"And you! Willmah." Dargen turned to his side.

"You will be punished with the highest punishment! But you will not be beheaded. You will be persecuted lifelong for your treachery and that young man too." He looked closely at Dan's eyes which were hidden behind

Willmah. After Dargen's words, a group of security guards came in and arrested Willmah and Dan, who refused to excuse themselves because they realized that their punishment was too mild for their sins. And everyone watched as they both got out and Dargen approached the table. All two connoisseurs and Adrian followed him.

"Dear friends, dear family!" said Dargen, in a very warm and calm voice.

"Our core service has lost its way and we have forgotten what the University is doing and for whom. As we have been debating and understanding what was happening here our people are falling apart, and we have to start looking for the answers to all the questions right there, and please find the worthy people who will join our ranks." And at the end of the speech Dargen looked at Adrian, and from Dargen's gaze everyone looked on him too.

"Me!" said Ad half – surprised.

"But I wasn't even a member of the University. Besides that I'd better be out there than sitting here." Adrian concluded in confusion.

"You are young, but you have lived as much as few have lived here to reach here," replied Dargen.

"Excuse me dear Dargen, but I have to deny you." And thinking for a while he continued.

"The service is not for me, I am used to flying freely."

"It's your decision! son." And getting closer to Adrian Dargen continued. "But even if you wish you will not be able to go far from your roots." Dargen said with a smile on his face.

"I'll still try to enjoy my life before joining my roots." Adrian joked, and during that time, the conference room was filled with a lot of positive energy that bestowed feelings of hope and happiness. Karma walked a bit ahead and whispered to Dargen.

"And what about Vam, what would you order them to do to him?" Getting even closer to Dargen.

"He may have made mistakes, but he accepted them."

"Hmm…," Dargen thought about Karma's words for a moment.

"Vam will stay on the board but will not be a Connoisseur anymore!" And giving a little rest to his word and following in the concerned eyes of everybody he continued.

"He will go to another service!"

"And what a service?" Randolph inquired.

"He will head and improve Sarhat." And feeling the stunned look on everyone.

"I hope he will manage to do whatever Valmar could not manage to do." Then Dargen approached the candle on the table, he looked at the white candle for a long time, he saw a reflection of the light of the torch hung on the wall and smiled.

Please review and provide your

Feedback

Thank You!

www.ingramcontent.com/pod-product-compliance
Lightning Source LLC
Chambersburg PA
CBHW070630310726
48982CB00001B/237
9781678006242